MYSTERY AT THE OLD STAMP MILL

C. Burkley

DEDICATION

For my husband, Craig,
who loves history,
and our four children, but me the most.
Thank you for helping me
fulfill my passion for writing.

ACKNOWLEDGMENTS

Thanks to my student, Matt Dryden; to Wally Marks of the Highway 50-95 Rock Shop in Fallon, Nevada; and to Bob Trussell, commander of the Lassen County (California) Search and Rescue Team.

Many thanks to the employees and volunteers at Plumas Eureka State Park in Johnsville, California, and to the volunteers at the Kentucky Mine Museum in Sierra City, California. Special thanks to Karen Donaldson, director of the Kentucky Mine Museum. These Sierra parks are treasures because of all of you.

MYSTERY AT THE OLD STAMP MILL

JANET HOLM MCHENRY

Chariot VICTOR
PUBLISHING
A DIVISION OF COOK COMMUNICATIONS

ANNIE SHEPARD MYSTERIES
Mystery at the Fairgrounds
Secret of the Locked Trunk
Mystery at the Old Stamp Mill

Designer: Andrea Boven
Cover Illustration: Rick Johnson

CIP information available upon request.

2 3 4 5 6 7 8 9 10 01 00 99 98 97

Chariot Books is an imprint of ChariotVictor Publishing,
a division of Cook Communications, Colorado Springs, Colorado 80918
Cook Communications, Paris, Ontario
Kingsway Communications, Eastbourne, England

CONTENTS

1

MISSING!

I slammed the gate to Grandma Rose's front walk. That was dumb. It wasn't Grandma Rose's fault.

I looked at the report card in my hand. It was my fault. But maybe she'd know what to do. . . .

"Annie!" Grandma Rose burst through the front door. "Just who I need to see! Have I got a case for you!"

A case? I folded up the report card and stuck it in my back jeans pocket. A case was a lot more important than a dumb old history grade.

"What's the matter, Gram?" I pulled my little spiral notebook and pen out of my ski jacket. I always carried them with me, ever since the first two cases of the After School Sleuths.

"John is missing! Mr. Cornwall that is. He never went to work today at the museum. His assistant just called me."

She dabbed her eyes with her rose-printed apron. Everything Grandma Rose wore was rose something.

John Cornwall was Grandma Rose's new gentleman friend—they had met at church. He was the museum director in Mountain Center, and in the two months I had known him, I had decided he was pretty okay. After all, Grandpa Geno had died years ago, and I knew Grandma Rose was lonely.

I pulled open the screen door. "Let's go inside, Gram." Wispy November clouds were blowing through that Friday afternoon with the threat of something bigger coming for our three-day weekend. The steep Sierra peaks all around our small mountain valley hid telltale weather signs from us, but a new crispness hinted at snow.

I shivered off my chill in Grandma Rose's cozy, woodstove-heated kitchen.

"Tea?" She poised the teapot over a cup and saucer on the round, cloth-covered table in front of me.

I nodded. "Now, fill me in on the details." I took notes as she explained that John Cornwall had not called or shown up at the museum. He always opened up the museum promptly at 8:30 after a half-hour coffee chat with friends at the Cattails Cafe.

"Dora, the guide at the museum, is beside herself. She even went to his home—no sign of him." Grandma Rose stared at her tea.

I began making a mental checklist. "Maybe he just had an appointment or something. When did you see him last?"

"We shared supper here two nights ago—Wednesday— before Bible group. He brought stew. I threw it in with my soup and we called it 'stoup.'" She laughed. "An appropriate name—it was pretty bad."

"And did he mention a doctor's appointment out of town or anything? Maybe he went to Reno on errands." I jotted down "Reno?" in my notebook.

"No, but that gives me an idea." Grandma Rose stood up and took off her apron. "He has an appointment book. Maybe it's at the museum or his home. Let's go!"

It didn't take us long to drive the few blocks to John Cornwall's small, yellow frame house. A friendly beagle barked his importance at us behind the neatly trimmed waist-high hedge. We entered through the aluminum gate, and the dog rushed to Grandma Rose's side, and waited for her pat.

"Where's your papa, Rusty?" she asked as she scratched his head. He whined as if he understood. "If John doesn't turn up by suppertime," Grandma Rose said to me, "I'd better bring this fellow to my house and take care of him."

We walked up concrete steps to a small porch. Grandma Rose knocked on the door. No answer. She knocked again, opening the door a bit. "John?"

Many people in our small town left their houses unlocked; John was no exception. We slowly looked through the house, each going a different direction. I went over my mental checklist. Maybe he'd had an accident. Maybe he'd had a heart attack. I kept my list to myself. I knew Grandma Rose probably had her own.

We walked all the way through the house, meeting again in the living room. No sign of John Cornwall. I looked over the masculine room—two large brown leather chairs, a TV set, and three trunks that served as end tables. He restored trunks—we'd learned that in our last case.

Our case? Oops! Here I was investigating without my two new friends, Maria and Alia. Together we had formed the motto: Sleuths After School Serving You"—SASSY! We made a great team. It was a lot more fun than eighth grade at Mountain Center Middle School and stuff like . . . history. I made a note for the mental checklist: Call M. and A.

Grandma Rose's and my eyes came to rest at the same time on a large wooden desk in the back corner of the room. Bills, letters, and cut-out articles all rested in separate, neat piles. We carefully peeked through them and the drawers of the desk.

I looked at Grandma Rose. "No appointment book."

She nodded. "Maybe it's at the museum."

But just at that moment, Rusty began barking. A louder, more threatening bark. Footsteps strained the porch boards. And then a heavy knock sounded at the door.

2

JUST THE TICKET?

My stomach swallowed my heart for a moment until I saw that it was Deputy Sheriff John Smithee. Grandma Rose opened the door to his puzzled, "Who are . . . I'm looking for John Cornwall."

"I am Rose Martoni, his friend. We were . . . are you? . . ."

"We got a call from the museum lady. He's missing, she told us. Have you seen him?"

"No, sir. My granddaughter, Anne, and I were just looking for his appointment book to see if we could track down his agenda for today. We didn't find anything."

The officer took out his own notebook. "You've checked everything here? Notes on the kitchen table or by the telephone?" He didn't wait for an answer. "Mind if I look around?" Again, he didn't wait but started for the kitchen.

I had a question. "Deputy Smithee? Is this a missing

person case already? I thought you guys had to wait forty-eight hours or something."

"Yup and nope, little lady. But you're not so little, are you?"

I blushed. I was five-feet, eight. Definitely not a little lady. I flipped back my growing-out brown hair, which always seemed to get in my way unless it was tied up.

The deputy finished sizing me up. "Aren't you the Shepard girl? Your parents own the feed store? You write for the newspaper once in a while."

I nodded, blushing again. I wasn't sure if any of that was good or bad. My parents had recently fled their L.A. law offices for small-town living. I was getting used to life in a one-traffic-light town.

"Anyway," he continued, "a recent California law mandates that we investigate all missing person reports immediately. There are a lot of weirdos out there—you never know what can happen."

I grimaced, hoping Grandma Rose hadn't heard that last remark. Those unspoken possibilities—kidnapping, assault, even murder—had already been on my mind.

I glanced at John Cornwell's desk again. Maybe there was a clue there—an appointment reminder or letter or something. I thumbed through the articles he had neatly clipped. They all related to gold mining. Not so strange. As the museum's curator, he was interested in all aspects of California history. On the bottom of the pile was a blue spiral-bound book, *Location and Patenting of Mining Claims and Mill Sites in California*, with a recent receipt for $9.47 attached to it. Now that was strange. Why would he be interested in an actual claim?

"Grandma Rose?" I showed her the book and articles.

"Oh, that." She smiled, taking the book. "He's gotten interested in gold panning, of all things. Maybe it relates to his past."

I nodded knowingly. I knew his family had once been active in gold mining. But John Cornwall a gold miner? It just didn't seem to suit him. A stack of old books was a lucky strike to him, not a few flakes in a gold pan.

Deputy Smithee peered over our shoulders. "Gold mining, eh? Now there's a dangerous business."

"Dangerous?" It didn't seem to me that swishing a pan of sand and water was that risky.

"You bet. First, a guy can lose his footing and drown. The Sierra River is pretty swift in places. And it's getting mighty cold out. He a good swimmer?"

"Yes," said Grandma Rose, "he's quite capable." She fingered the large buttons on her rose-colored wool coat.

The deputy removed his hat and scratched his receding hairline. "Well, not much you can do if you fall and hit your head. Or if someone else hits your head."

"Someone else?" I asked.

"Like a claim jumper," he said, "or someone who thinks you're jumping his claim. They can be mighty feisty, those miners. Very particular about how it's all done. Don't want anyone horning in on their territory. Supposed to be all legal-like—that book should spell it out. But sometimes legal isn't what happens."

Grandma Rose set her lips and fingered the coat buttons

again.

"Now, ma'am can you give me a description of Mr. Cornwall? And his vehicle?"

I listened halfheartedly while Grandma Rose told the deputy about John Cornwall. I knew he drove a small blue pickup truck. He was about five feet ten, white-haired with smiley wrinkles. He was fairly strong and energetic for a man in his mid-seventies, especially for someone who'd had a stroke. The telltale sign was a twitch in his left eye, which, I admit, had sort of bothered me at first.

I fished through the wastebasket next to his desk. Ripped-open envelopes and catalogs. An empty postage stamp book. And a receipt. It read:

Thank you for your donation
Senior: $2.00
Sierra-Eureka Stamp Mill Museum

What on earth was a "stamp mill"? And why was John Cornwall visiting it? Maybe this was a clue. I stuck the receipt in my pocket. Maybe Grandma Rose would know.

3

MUSEUM MOSEYING

Even though the deputy had already been there, Grandma Rose and I decided to check out the museum. We were cruising along in her most-cool brown-and-white '57 Chevy when she said, "Anne, dear, it just occurred to me . . . did you have a reason for visiting this afternoon? I was so wrapped up in my own business, I didn't think to ask."

"Uh, yeah, Grandma Rose." Frankly, I'd forgotten too. I reached into my jeans pocket and held out my report card. "It's this. I got a 'D' in history. Mom and Dad are going to flip."

Grandma Rose was deadeyeing the road. "You're right. You know they both majored in history in college."

"Believe me, I know. They remind me every time I complain about the subject."

Grandma Rose pulled into a parking slot next to the

museum, stopped the car, and turned toward me. "Are you trying your hardest, Anne?"

I sighed. "Not exactly."

"Are you trying at all?"

I sighed again. "Not exactly."

This time, she sighed. "Well, we'll just have to get John to help you. History is his subject too. And he knows how to make it fun."

I snickered. "Grandma Rose. History and fun? Isn't that one of those things my English teacher just told us about, an oxymoron? Two things that don't go together?"

Grandma Rose laughed. "Well, today it might be. But, look, aren't those your friends?"

Heading up the museum sidewalk were my sleuthing partners. "Hey, Maria, Alia!" I ran to meet them.

"Hi, Annie!" they said in unison, then turned toward each other and giggled. They always said the same thing at the same time. It was weird, but I was getting used to it.

"What are you guys doing here?"

"History project, Annie," said Maria, the dark-haired one with the athletic build.

"Remember?" said Alia, the short, skinny blonde. "It's due in a week. We came to the museum to check things out."

Grandma Rose had caught up with us. "Hi, Grandma Rose!" they chimed, giggling again.

"Well, forget the history paper," I said. "We have a new case. John Cornwall is missing."

After answering their one hundred and one questions on the way in, we met Dora at the door. "Welcome to the

Mountain County Museum . . ." she began.

I gave Dora the "cut" sign with my hand across my neck. Dora's monologue was like a telephone salesman's—it was hard to stop. "Dora, we're here about Mr. Cornwall. We'd like to look at his desk and see if we can find any clues about where he might be."

Dora wrung her hands. "It's such a mystery, such a mystery. He's never done this before in the thirty-five years, two months, and five days we've worked together. He always lets me know where he'll be. I'm so worried about him. He's . . . he's all I've got." Her eyes darted left, then right, then squared on Grandma Rose, and she pursed her lips ever so slightly.

He's all she's got? That was a weird remark. I looked at Grandma Rose. Her eyes had widened, but otherwise she was not responding.

"We're all concerned, Dora," I said. "That's why we want to look at his appointment book."

"Well, I don't know," she said. "You're not relatives or anything."

"Well, almost," blurted Maria. "I mean, Mrs. Martoni's about married to the guy."

Grandma Rose turned two hundred and two shades of rose. "Well, not exactly, Maria, but we are good friends."

Dora stopped wringing her hands and instead crossed her arms over her chest. "How good?"

I gave Grandma Rose head and eyebrow signals that meant "distract her." She picked right up on it and slowly walked around Dora so that the docent's back was to Mr. Cornwall's desk. Maria, Alia, and I quietly inched our way to the desk. I pointed to the trash basket, and my friends started combing through its contents. I looked over the top of his desk.

Like his desk at home, it was orderly, with piles of papers clipped together. A large calendar with leather corners covered much of the top surface.

Only weekday activities were marked, with special tours noted for school classes and tour groups. At first nothing unusual stood out. Then I noticed it. Every Thursday Mr. Cornwall had the same four o'clock tour. Why would the same group want to tour the museum every week? It didn't make sense. The tour group's name was "S.E.S.M.M." Or was it a tour? Those initials were familiar. . . .

From my jacket pocket I pulled out the receipt that I'd found in John Cornwall's trash. At the bottom it read, "Sierra-Eureka Stamp Mill Tour." That was what S.E.S.M.M. meant: Sierra-Eureka Stamp Mill Museum. John Cornwall had visited the stamp mill museum last night.

I looked over at Grandma Rose. She was nodding while Dora was alternately wringing and crossing her hands. Oh, boy. Now I really had to cut off Dora! We had to get to the Stamp Mill Museum, whatever and wherever it was, right away!

4

HELP FROM HENRY

"Bye" was all I told Dora, as Maria and Alia whooshed Grandma Rose out the door and into her car. A minute later I had spilled my find to the three of them.

"I know where that is," said Grandma Rose as she backed her car out and headed toward the highway.

"So what would John Cornwall want with stamps?" I asked, looking at the receipt. "Did he collect them?"

"They're not postage stamps," said Alia. "They're big metal stamping things at the mill by the gold mine."

Grandma Rose nodded. "That's right. The stamp mill is the place where the mill workers crushed the quartz rock taken from the mountain to get to the gold. The county park is just on the edge of town—up the hill against the mountain."

I nodded. I'd seen the signs, but there was a lot I hadn't yet explored in Mountain Center. Mom and Dad worked all the time at their business. Here we were right in the middle of mountain vacation paradise with no time to enjoy it. Ha! Paradise. I still thought paradise was where we used to live—halfway between Disneyland and the beach.

The Sierra-Eureka Stamp Mill Museum was just on the edge of town—a couple of winding road blocks away. A good challenge for my new mountain bike, I figured.

Grandma Rose pulled into the parking lot, empty except for one pickup truck at the far edge of the lot. The museum looked like the log house from "Bonanza"—a big covered front porch and large logs layered one on top of the other. We got out of the car and walked up the stone pathway. Maria easily pulled open the heavy wooden door, and we walked up to the reverse L-shaped counter. A gray-haired man wearing a red plaid shirt and overalls sat in a wooden chair reading a book. His name badge said "Henry."

He started at our advance. "Well, excuse me, ladies. Didn't hear you come in. Better turn this thing up a notch." He fiddled with something behind his ear, and then smiled. "There. What can I do you for?"

I cleared my throat. "We're looking for a friend of ours. His name is John Cornwall. We think he's visited here a few times—perhaps even yesterday afternoon. Have you seen him?"

The man scratched his nose a moment. "Well, sure. Nice feller. Comes here every Thursday. And I believe. . .yep, see here in the register. . . here's his name. John Cornwall. Yep, he was here yesterday." He scratched his nose again. "Come to think of it, he left his bicycle out front. I thought that was mighty strange, but I figgered he'd come back fer it. Let's go take a look."

We walked back out the front door to the side of the building where an empty bicycle rack stood.

"Funny," Henry said. "It was here this morning when I got here. Fella must've come and got it. Yep, that's it. Must've come and got it. I just missed him." He rested his thumbs in his overall bib. "Can I help with something else? Want a tour of the stamp mill? The last one of the day—the four o'clock one—just headed up the hill. You could still catch it."

I was itching. My folks didn't call me Curious Anne for nothing. "Sir, uh, Henry, what exactly does Mr. Cornwall do when he comes? You see, he hasn't been seen since you saw him yesterday, and we're trying to track him down."

"Well, come on in, ladies, and I'll show you." Henry escorted us to a back corner of the building adjacent to the office area. A large wooden table with a few chairs mostly filled the small room, which also held a bookcase stuffed with old books and a large dresser-thing with wide, shallow drawers.

There he showed us the diaries, old newspapers, and letters John Cornwall had been reading every Thursday, according to Henry, for the last two months. Like clockwork, he arrived shortly after four and read and took notes.

"Are these, by any chance, about mining?" Grandma Rose asked.

Henry scratched his nose again. "Do believe so, ma'am. All these books and papers here—they're open to the public. We don't keep track of what folks are reading They just can't take it with 'em. I couldn't point you to any one particular thing, but I do believe your friend was studying all kinds of things about local miners and the Sierra-Eureka Mining Company."

"That's all he did—come here and read?" I got out my little spiral book again and jotted some notes.

"Well, little lady, no. I think he's been on our tour a coupla times and some days, after he was done studying he'd say, 'Henry, think I'll go for a little hike.' Now, what do you think of that? 'A little hike' after bicyclin' all the way up this steep ol' hill. But then again some folks are into that fitness thing." He patted his sides. "Not me. I don't need that fitness stuff. Been fit as a fiddle since I dragged rock out of that ol' mountain. Fit as a fiddle." He coughed, first a tickling cough, then a big hacky one.

I grimaced as we walked away, saying our good-byes and thanks, heading out the door. Mining didn't strike me as a particularly healthy occupation. Granted, I didn't know much about it at that moment, but I had a feeling I was soon going to know a lot more.

5

A FIND

"That thing about the bike bothers me," I said as we drove back down the hill. "I mean, John leaves his bike there, then comes and gets it the next day? How did he get home? It just doesn't make sense."

"Unless, Anne dear, Mr. Henry is simply mistaken about seeing the bicycle." Grandma Rose was taking the trip back down the hill in slow motion.

"Or not seeing it." I wasn't convinced that Henry was all there. He couldn't hear; maybe his sight wasn't all that good either. He seemed nice enough, but something had made me feel uneasy about our museum visit. I was learning to expect the unexpected and not trust initial impressions.

"Grandma Rose," I said, "does John Cornwall have any enemies?"

"No, absolutely not. He's the kindest man you could meet. He drives for Meals on Wheels every lunch hour, you know. He ... he ..." She bit her lip. Was there a tear forming behind her spectacles?

She got quiet, so we all got quiet. Then I noticed that we were pulling up to Grandma Rose's home. I had thought she would drop us each off.

"Girls, I hope you don't mind if I just leave you here." She turned off the engine and turned to us. "I'm not feeling too well. I'm a little dizzy, light-headed. Maybe all of this is a bit much for me." Grandma Rose reached for her handbag.

"No problem, Grandma Rose," Maria and Alia said in sync.

"Could I use your phone?" I opened the car door. "Link has been harassing me all week about waxing his car. It's payment for a loan." Link—short for Lincoln—was my very perturbing teenaged brother.

Grandma Rose nodded, motioning me toward her gate. Then she stopped. "I just thought of something. John did mention the other evening that he had been getting harassing phone calls. In fact, he bought an answering machine so he could screen them."

"Grandma Rose!" I grabbed her shoulders. "There could be a message on his machine. We should. . . No, you go get some rest. Maria, Alia, and I will go check his house again.

"We'll give you a call when we get there." I started off, then stopped and turned. "Umm, Grandma Rose . . . could you please call Link and tell him I'm right on that wax deal?"

She looked faraway for a moment, and I could feel a quotation coming. "Yet moons swiftly wax again after they have waned."

I put my hands on my hips. "And that's? . . ."

"Horace." She smiled. Grandma Rose, a retired English teacher, had a memory that wouldn't quit. Quotations were her specialty. "No last name. Just Horace."

"Like Sting?" Alia asked.

Grandma Rose giggled. "No, dear—more like Homer."

Maria and Alia looked a little puzzled, but I sighed in relief. Grandma Rose was probably just tired. "Okay, Grandma Rose, I won't keep putting Link off. Go take a rest. We'll call you soon."

It was only a few blocks to John Cornwall's home. In fact, everything in Mountain Center was just a few blocks from everything else. The whole town was about a mile long, with the courthouse and museum in the middle surrounded by an old-fashioned downtown and a small supermarket center on the west end and a wood mill and the county fairgrounds on the east end. To the south, up against the mountain, was the stamp mill and mine. On the north side of town was a small farming valley.

In a few minutes Maria, Alia, and I were at John Cornwall's. Rusty greeted us with friendly slurps. We found food inside the back door and fed and watered him.

Outside again, Maria had the same thought I did. "Annie, there's no bike here."

"Or car," said Alia. "Doesn't he have a blue pickup?"

"Yes," I said. "Let's check the garage." We followed cement strips the width of tires down the right side of his house to his garage, which was closed. I peeked through a small window. "It's here! Let's check it out."

I opened a door on the left side of the garage. A musty dampness greeted my nose. I flipped the light switch and stepped inside. Maria and Alia followed, and we all surveyed the garage for a moment.

John Cornwall was an orderly man. A pegboard covered the back wall, with tools hanging in graduated sizes from left to right, largest to smallest. This was a man who did everything just so. He kept appointments at the same time each week. He delivered meals faithfully. He attended church every Sunday. How could such a man just vanish? At that moment, I somehow knew that his disappearance was not of his own doing. I opened the driver's side of the pickup and sat behind the wheel. The bench seat was empty. I reached over and opened the glove compartment. A small, clear plastic folder held only car papers. Again, everything was in order. Not like my family's cars, which usually held telltale signs of takeout meals and scattered cassette tapes.

"Annie, what's that?" Maria was pointing to a pocket on the driver's door. Protruding from it was a small black zippered briefcase.

I opened it slowly and muffled a soft gasp. Inside were a yellow legal pad and two black, leather-bound books. One read "Appointments." The other, "Journal."

6

A WARNING

We hustled back to the house, entering through the back door this time. We still had to check the message machine, and I wanted to call Grandma Rose. It wasn't hard to find the new white phone message machine on the old green-tiled kitchen counter. There were three messages waiting. Maria and Alia gathered around as I pushed the playback button and pulled out my notepad and pencil.

"Beep. Hello, John. This is Rose. I have leftover stoup from last night. Call me when you're home from work."

"Beep. Hi. Rose again. It's eight forty-five. Just wondered if you're all right."

"Beep. Cornwall, stay away from the river! You owe me something first!" Cursing followed, interrupted by a coarse, deep cough.

I turned toward Maria and Alia and wondered if I looked

as pale as they did.

"I...don't think we should tell your grandma about that message, Annie." Maria was outlining the mottled floor tile with her tennis-shoed toe.

"I think we should tell the police," said Alia. "This is getting creepy. And you know I don't do creepy well."

"Okay. I agree with you both. I just need to call Grandma Rose and let her know about finding his portfolio and things."

I dialed her number. One ring, two rings. A full ten rings later, still no answer.

"Weird." I shrugged my shoulders at my two friends. "Not home."

We agreed that maybe Grandma Rose was resting. I made a mental note to have my parents check on her. It was getting late, so we parted ways, each heading for home. Before we left we flipped through a photo album on the coffee table and took out two photos of John Cornwall. Maria agreed to take one and ask about Cornwall at businesses on her way home. Alia would do the same. I thought that was pretty gutsy of Alia, who normally wouldn't even talk to a grocery checker.

I walked to the east end of town to where our old two-story house sat at the end of a short dirt road bordering the fairgrounds. Daylight savings time had dropped in about two weeks before, and it was close to dark. I hoped Mom and Dad wouldn't freak—after all, I had told them I was going to Grandma Rose's house after school.

That reminded me: I'd forgotten all about my report

card. I gulped. Grounded-ville. As I walked up the front steps and opened the squeaky front door, I could just about guess what they'd say and do.

But greeting me—and I use that word most loosely—in the front hallway was my brother Link, armed with portable phone in one hand and a slice of pizza in the other. He looked like Mom's and Grandma Rose's Italian side of the family—tall, thin, dark. "You're dead meat." He took a bite. "No, not you, Crystal. The squirt . . . Yeah, she's home. . . . No, I don't think she knows."

Another bite. "Hey, Squirt. Did you know Grandma Rose is in the hospital? She called Dad at the store. He just took her. She fainted or something—I don't know. By the way, your history teacher—Millerton?—called. Says he wants to explain your first-quarter grade. Dead meat, kid.

Grandma Rose in the hospital? She didn't look too great when we left her house, but . . . I slumped to the floor. Now I wasn't feeling too good either. I watched Link start up the stairs, two at a time. Brothers! How could he just go on as if nothing had happened?

I threw a stray tennis shoe at him. "Hey, get off the phone, will you? Mom and Dad might be trying to call or something."

Link paused midway up the stairs, shrugged, and said good-bye to Crystal. He turned around. "I've got a better idea, Squirt. Let's go to the hospital."

You just can't figure out teenaged brothers. One minute they're running for Dope of the Year, the next minute they're halfway human. The hospital—on the north end of the business section—was a bumpy couple of minutes away in Link's pickup.

Mountain Center's hospital is not too complicated. You go in one door if it's not serious. You go in another if it is. We went in the second one. There in a nook outside the small emergency room was a waiting area, where Mom and Dad were on the edge of their chairs, slumped over.

"Annie! Link!" Mom—slim and trim—wore jeans better than I did. She gave us both hugs. Dad did, too, and I brushed a piece of hay out of his rumpled sandy blond hair. His eyes sagged behind his gold wire frames.

We quickly found out that the doctor wanted to admit Grandma Rose for the night. She was going to be all right. With the stresses of the day—which Mom and Dad had just learned about—she had neglected to eat and passed out shortly after we had left.

"What's that, Annie?" Dad pointed to the zippered case under my arm. In all the confusion I had forgotten I was still clutching it.

"It's..."

"...John's portfolio!" Grandma Rose finished my sentence as a nurse pushed her in a wheelchair out of the emergency room. The sight of the I.V. bag and tube taped to her arm startled me, but otherwise she looked better than she had when we had parted ways.

"Maria, Alia, and I found it in his truck, Grandma Rose. It was in his garage. It's got his appointment book and journal in it. Do you want to look through them?"

Grandma Rose reached out and squeezed my hand.

"No, dear, you're the detective. Go ahead and see what you can find out. And could you folks fetch John's dog and look after him? I'm going to be laid up here a while."

We walked Grandma Rose to her room around the corner, then said good night. The doctor—a round, older man—chatted with Mom and Dad a moment. As I walked back down the hall, I was relieved that Grandma Rose hadn't remembered to ask about the answering machine.

I was almost to the emergency hall outside door when I heard, "Hello, Annie." It was a man's voice, coming from the waiting area. There sat Mr. Millerton, my eighth grade social studies teacher, wet from his midsection down and holding his right elbow.

7

COINCIDENCES?

Just my luck. At the same moment, Mom and Dad and Link turned the hall corner. I considered saying a very quick hello and rushing my family out the door, but Mr. Millerton was quicker.

"Hi, I'm Steve Millerton, Annie's history teacher. I'd shake hands, but I can't do that right now." He winced. "I did a number on my elbow. Slipped at the river." He did look a mess. His jeans and work boots were dripping, and his large '49er sweatshirt was wet from the waist down. He sniffed and brushed his nose with his left arm, then covered his move by smoothing his thick brown hair.

Dad smiled. "That's okay. I'm Mark Shepard and this is my wife, Kate, and our son, Lincoln."

Mr. Millerton turned to cough, then cleared his voice. "Excuse me—allergies, I think. Didn't I speak with you this afternoon, Lincoln?"

"Oh, yeah. Mom, he wants to talk with you about Annie's history grade."

I looked away and mumbled, "My favorite subject."

Dad looked surprised. "Anne? Wasn't this report card day? Do we have something to talk about at home?"

I nodded, reached into my back pocket, and handed over the report card. Dad unfolded it, and he, Mom, and Link scanned it quickly.

"A 'D' in history?" Link was definitely not diplomatic. And Mom and Dad did not look happy.

To my great fortune, a nurse stepped over. "Mr. Millerton, the doctor can see you now."

"You can give me a call at school or at home. Annie just needs a little motivating. Nothing we can't all work out together." Mr. Millerton waved with his good hand and walked into the emergency room.

I grimaced. The report card was out of the bag. And the drive home was not a pretty scene, even with our stop at John's house to collect one very lonely dog. First Dad got on my case. Then Mom. It was the same old thing. History is our favorite subject. We majored in history in college. History is Link's best subject. Blah, blah, blah.

I tuned into another brain station. *God, what good is history anyway? It's over and done with. Who cares who fought what battle in what year? It's just dead people stuff. I'm more interested in now—like John Cornwall's disappearance. Don't You agree?*

I geared up for Grounded-ville but was surprised when Mom and Dad changed the subject. They wanted to know about John Cornwall. So I explained the events of the afternoon, even the phone message. Dad thought everyone was overreacting and that John Cornwall was probably out of town on museum business. Mom wasn't so sure—she's mostly ruled by her heart like Grandma Rose, even though her legal background sometimes bends her toward only weighing hardrock evidence. They agreed we should wait things out until the next day. Surely, Mom said, he'd turn up by then, if not later this evening.

I was dying to dig into John Cornwall's journal and appointment book, but decided for diplomacy's sake that I'd help throw together dinner. The Shepards' specialty is M&M+S. That's not a new kind of candy. It's Microwaved Meal Plus Salad. Mom calls it "Survival Food." We each pick out what we want, line it up at the microwave, and throw mixed salad greens in a bowl. We do try and eat together, and I'm in charge of the prayer.

Since I was the microwave manager, Link had to clean up. In my room I flopped down on my blue quilt and opened up John's case while Rusty watched me with interest. I felt really weird—as if I were going through someone's underwear drawer or something. But I knew that if there were clues to John Cornwall's disappearance, they'd be in one of those two books.

I thumbed through the appointment book. It had a page for each day, with the hours listed and spaces for appointments. It seemed to have the same listings as his desk calendar did at the museum. I remembered the school tours. But it also had weekend dates. "Ice Cream Social Fund-raiser" written for a September Saturday. "Movie/2:20" noted for an October Sunday. Nothing seemed to be out of the ordinary.

Then I noticed something. On October 5, a Saturday, John Cornwall had written "Steve Millerton/river" next to 8 a.m. I flipped the pages, scanning them quickly. The next Saturday, the 12th, at 8 a.m. it read "Millerton." It was the same for the next two Saturdays at the same time. I flipped into November. The first Saturday, November 2, simply had a big "X" over the whole day. I looked ahead to November 9—which would be tomorrow—and it was also crossed out. So were the next two Saturdays.

I got the portable phone from Mom and Dad's room down the hall. John Cornwall had met Mr. Millerton at the river four Saturdays in a row. Maria and Alia had to hear about that.

"Alia, you won't believe this."

"Annie? You won't believe mine either."

"Okay—you first."

"I stopped at the Quick Save on the way home—you know, to ask about Mr. Cornwall. And—you'd be proud of me, Annie—I asked the clerk there about him and showed him the picture and all. And she didn't know anything, but— you're not going to believe this. His bicycle was leaning against the building."

"His bicycle?" She was right. I couldn't believe it. "Wait a minute. How do you know what John Cornwall's bicycle looks like?"

"Well, I don't, actually. But it's got a Mountain County

Museum sticker on it."

I scratched my head. "It could be. Did you ask someone about it?"

"Sure. I asked the clerk if she knew whose bike it was. She said no, and that it had been there since late morning or so. I rode it home—it's here at my house. Weird, huh?"

"About as weird as mine," I said. I told Alia about John Cornwall and Mr. Millerton and about seeing our teacher at the hospital.

"Why was he there?" she asked.

"He said he hurt his elbow or something. He fell at the river."

"The river again?"

I gulped. He had fallen at the river. John Cornwall was missing. And it all had something to do with the stamp mill or the Sierra-Eureka Mining Co.—which at that moment I realized were adjacent to the river! Maybe I needed to pay another hospital visit—to see Mr. Millerton. Could he have had something to do with the disappearance of John Cornwall? Suddenly I felt microwaved pocket pizza rising to the occasion . . . and that was not a good thing.

8

EAVES-READING

I called Maria, but she hadn't learned anything. She had, however, gone to her dad's graphic design office and made up a MISSING! poster. She had scanned in the photo and made copies for us to distribute the next day.

I cut our conversation short. John Cornwall's journal was beckoning to me. I flopped on my bed again, opened the journal to the first page, and I started reading.

September 30

Are the fragments of my life amalgamating—coming together like mercury and gold? I just learned that Sarah Lahti Millerton is my real mother—birth mother, they say. Elizabeth and Philip Cornwall did a fine job raising me in Placerton. I always knew I was adopted, but I never had the desire to know the circumstances.

Until now. Now that I've met Sarah, I also want to know what happened to her husband, Albert Millerton. My father. Months before I was born, in March 1921, he disappeared. There were rumors. some say he hit a vein of gold in the mountain. Some say there was a mining accident. But it was well known that there was a dispute between Albert and the Lahti family who owned Sierra-Eureka Mining Co., about the ownership of the claim and the mining company. I'd like to know. Sarah, my mother, is ill with Alzheimer's disease. Perhaps knowing the truth—if I could make her understand—could put her troubled mind to rest. Perhaps it would mine, as well.

There are letters and diaries at the stamp mill museum, the site of the historic Sierra-Eureka Mining Co. I'm going to see if any are from the Millerton family—my family.

His beautiful handwriting impressed me. It was prettier than any grammar school teacher's I'd seen. I turned the page.

October 3

What a productive day! Henry Cubbins, a volunteer at the Sierra-Eureka County Park museum, pointed me toward a whole collection of letters and diaries of miners and other settlers of these parts. Nothing's too organized, but it seems likely that there will be something from the Millerton family. I'm hopeful.

I ran into a couple of other folks. Carl Taylor is the museum director. "Slave," he said, is a better term. I know what he means. I have to clean the bathrooms too. He'll give me a tour of the stamp mill. I understand the mine shafts are not open anymore. Pity. I bet there's history in them—some say bodies from cave-in accidents.

Then on the way home I ran into Steve Millerton, a history teacher, who was panning gold at the Sierra River just below the park. When I happened to mention that I'd always been interested in panning, he said he'd get me started. We're going to meet on Saturday mornings until I get the feel for it. I didn't say anything about it to him, but I wonder if we're related. Can't be too many Millertons around.

I was reading Scripture last night, and found this verse: "For you have heard my vows, O God; you have given me the heritage of those who fear your name." Psalm 61:5. Thank you, God, that even if I do not find out about my father's past, I have a heritage in Your family.

October 5
First day of panning. It's a lot more strenuous than I thought—digging out rock and so forth. Steve is a bit mysterious—friendly, yet reserved. He doesn't think we're related—doesn't know of my mother

October 10
Carl Taylor—the stamp mill curator—was a bit strange. When he found out that I was reading letters related to the Millerton family, he hemmed and hawed and said, no, I couldn't read them. I needed to use gloves to look over "his materials" as he called them. I should have thought of that—the oils on my hands damaging them.

I spent the rest of the afternoon poking around the various mine entrances. One near the stamp mill is obviously closed off with plywood. But another—one much higher up and off the trail for tourists—appears to be open. Why would Carl Taylor tell me they all were closed? And why was he so abrupt? I think Annie would have told him to "chill."

October 12
I think I've made fifty cents from panning. Every likely spot seems to have been panned out. Why is it that Millerton, then, seems to be doing so well? Practice, I guess.

October 17
An odd thing happened. The collection of letters and diaries at the stamp mill museum has dwindled from dozens of things that filled the drawers of that great cabinet to just a handful. Whatever remains has nothing to do with mining or folks involved with the Sierra-Eureka Mining Co. The curator, Carl Taylor, was gone for the day. I'm going to try and call him before the weekend.

October 19
A crusty young man with leathery skin cussed me out at the river today. He said I was working his placer claim and to leave it alone. Millerton had wandered away upstream. I decided to quit for the day. I have to find out the law about filing claims. When I got home, I got two nasty phone calls—anonymous. One said, "Stay away from the mining company." The other said, "Stay away from the river." Odd.

October 24
A few letters made it back to the museum. Nothing yet. While

I was exploring the mine entrance up the mountain, a tour guide—a younger guy, not workout—strong, but work strong—yelled at me. Told me to stay on the park trails—the mine was off limits. He was not nice about it. He wore a necklace of rattlesnake rattles.

October 26
Millerton didn't show up. I piddled around the river a while until I spotted the crusty fellow. I decided to leave rather than face a conflict with him. I had another threatening phone call today. An answering machine could take care of that.

October 31
Halloween day, and a ghost from my past turned up at the museum. I found a letter from my mother to her mother.
Dear Mother:
I hope Father has forgiven me for marrying Albert. He has not come home; the townfolk say he's dead. I do not know how they could know that. I have given birth. It was a little sooner than the doctor expected. There were two babies, Mother, Charles William, a healthy boy, and Anne Leah. She was dead at birth. I cried for two days straight. I kept her in a shoebox on top of the piano and when I stopped crying, I buried her in our backyard. It is a nice house, Mother. I wish you and Father would visit us.
            Love, Sarah

November 2
It rained today. The washout off the hill opened up a spot, and I actually found a nugget and a few flakes. It was half the size of

*a single piece of rice. I can imagine how miners "saw the elephant"—
experienced the highs and lows of the quest for golden riches. Another
low tonight—nasty messages on my machine. I should call the
sheriff.*

I turned the page. Nothing more. I made a list of what I
had learned:

1. John Cornwall had started gold panning with Mr.
Millerton's help.

2. John was researching the disappearance of his father
in 1921.

3. There was a dispute between his father and his mother's family about a gold claim and the mining company's
ownership.

4. His mother's family did not approve of his parents'
marriage.

5. Letters and diaries had disappeared from the museum.

My head was heavy on my arm. It was a lot to think about.
And Maria, Alia, and I had three hundred and three leads
to follow up tomorrow.

9

GOING BATTY

Maria's phone call woke me up Saturday morning. She, Alia and I would meet at the Cattails Cafe to put up the MISS-ING! posters. When I stumbled downstairs, I found a note next to cold French toast:

Annie—

Mom and I have gone to the feed store for the day. Rusty's been fed and has had a walk. I've already checked by John's house—no sign yet. The doctor wants to keep Grandma Rose for another day. Why don't you visit her? It's okay if you do some sleuthing around the museums, but carry the cell phone. We may need you.

Love,

Dad

I stuffed the phone in my backpack and headed out the kitchen door for my bike. I couldn't believe that Mom and Dad weren't sending me to the tower for my 'D' in history;

it seemed, in fact, that they had forgotten it. Maybe they were reserving punishment until they talked with Mr. Millerton. I smiled. In our first two cases, Mom and Dad hadn't taken our sleuthing too seriously. But now, it seemed, Dad was encouraging it.

I met up with Maria and Alia outside the cafe where they were leaning on their bikes. Actually, Alia was leaning on John Cornwall's bike. They showed me how they had already tacked a poster on a bulletin board next to the cafe's front door. Under his picture it read:

MISSING!

JOHN CORNWALL

Mountain County Museum Director

Call: 231-1416

I sighed. That was my phone number. Now I could get some weirdo phone calls. But I was the leader. I forced a grin.

"Thanks, Maria. Great poster."

After I showed the others John Cornwall's diary, we agreed that the best thing would be to retrace his steps on the afternoon of disappearance—Thursday.

Our first stop was the Mountain County Museum. Dora rushed toward us with her tiny pigeon-toed steps, coughing hoarsely.

"Any word? Any word?" Dora often repeated herself when nervous.

"We're following up a few leads, Dora," I said calmly. "We know that John was researching his family history at the Stamp Mill Museum and that he had taken up gold panning."

Dora wrung her hands in her white, starched apron.

"Oh, those are dangerous places—the stamp mill and the river. My cousin drowned in that river. And did you hear about the cave-in?"

"What cave-in?" we three chimed.

"There was a cave-in at an upper mine entrance above the stamp mill. It wasn't discovered until last night when they were closing up the park. A tour guide found it. It must have happened Thursday night. I warned John—Mr. C—about that place. I told him. I told him. Oh, he's all I've got, all I've got."

"That's where we're headed, Dora." I inched toward the door, and Maria and Alia did the same.

"Oh, my. Oh, my. Be careful. Be careful."

At the end of the walk Alia turned around and held up her hand like a traffic cop. "Are we crazy? He was threatened! He was warned! He was never heard of again! And we're walking right into the middle of it?"

"Nope," said Maria. "We're riding. Get on your bike, girl."

It took some good huffing and puffing to climb the mere quarter-mile to Sierra-Eureka County Park. By the time we greeted Henry at the front desk of the museum, we had zipped open our parkas, sweating.

"You little ladies are just in time for the ten o'clock tour.

"Tour?" I asked. "Of what?"

"Why, of the stamp mill, of course. And if you're out for a little exercise today, Butch will take you up the trail to the old mine entrances."

Maria looked interested. "Would that include the one that just caved in?"

"Now how did you know that?" He frowned. "Why, yes,

I suppose it does."

"How much does it cost?" Alia asked.

"Well, it being Local History Month, it doesn't cost a nickel for school kids. But you ladies aren't in school still, are you?" Henry's eyes twinkled.

Maria pulled me aside. "Annie, we can kill two assignments with one tour. Remember the history project? We can use the stamp mill tour as part of our research. And maybe we'll find a clue for the case, too."

Now that made sense. Minutes later we were hiking up the hill with Butch, a muscular young man with short-cropped, curly blond hair and a matching trimmed mustache. He wore a red pullover sweater, hiking boots, and an odd necklace made of pods.

"Welcome to the Sierra-Eureka Mining Company," he bellowed to our group of ten, including two tourist families with kids. You'll find our tour is cheaper than going to the gym and using the Stairmaster."

Butch led us to the first mine entrance. The sign over the timber—he called it a portal—said:

Tunnel No. 2

West Virginia Portal

I was hoping to get a glance inside, but it was completely blocked with a plywood covering.

"Can you get in there?" I asked.

"No, but we're hoping to get some grant money to clear out and shore up this tunnel. It's just one of nine tunnels in this mountain—some twenty-six miles altogether. A hundred years ago there were hundreds of men working here." He pointed toward the tunnel. "It was an entirely different world then. In fact, Mountain Center was once a booming city of forty thousand."

"Ten times what it is now?" Alia asked.

"That's right." Butch gave a slight nudge to an ore cart that sat on railroad-like tracks. It moved down the hill toward a narrow wooden bridge to the stamp mill. Another track led to the edge of a sharp cliff. "Let's follow the ore cart over the trestle to the stamp mill."

"That looks kind of scary," said Alia.

"It's safe now with handrails," said Butch, "but back then all of this was a very dangerous life." He pointed toward some equipment. "These drills were called widow makers—for a reason. And there were other accidents—with black powder and dynamite. The Pelton wheels—used to generate power through water—could knock a guy flat. Rock falling through chutes into the ore cars could miss its mark."

We had reached the stamp mill at its top floor—the hopper room. The ore car had reached its stopping point, too.

Butch motioned to me. "Now dump that car, please."

"Who me?"

"Go ahead—lift it."

I shrugged my shoulders, breathed out heavily, and gripped the ends of the car. Surprisingly it wasn't that heavy—probably a lever principle—and the car tipped easily. The rock clattered down into the building, sorted by screening into sizes. Butch led us down the stairs to the next level.

As we started down the dimmed, steep stairs, something fluttered past my face. "Ahhhh!" I jumped back and landed against Alia.

"Oh, don't mind him. It's just Bert."

"B-b-b-bert?" Alia was shaking.

"Bert the bat," said Butch. "He's a Townsend's Big-eared Bat—an endangered species. He and Ernestina live here. They're pretty cool. They can hover like hummingbirds to eat or move their young. Cute little things."

"Little things?" I said. "That was no little thing."

"About a foot in wing span. He won't bother you girls. He'd rather eat moths." Butch continued down the steps.

I didn't know quite what to make of our guide. He was polite, sometimes funny in a dry way, but not friendly. Our next stopping point down into the building was at the jaw crusher, Butch said. Eighty tons of rock a day flew down and through the metal jaws that crushed it. Mistakes could send enough rock flying to fill the room. Large leather belts spun quickly to move the machinery. "Back then there wasn't insurance. Men were careful. If you weren't, you could lose your life or, at the least, a few fingers."

I looked at Maria and Alia. Maybe John Cornwall had been here. Maybe in his search for clues about his family he had not been careful. There were trapdoors that led to storage bins deep in the building. No one would know if someone had come to some harm.

I hung back from the group and peeked into the nearest trapdoor. Squeak. Squeak. Squeak.

"Is that machinery running?" I asked.

"No," said Butch. "Just the bats."

10

SEARCH
AND RESCUE

Bats! I scurried back to the group. Butch was on a new subject. "The mine was closed for a few years at the turn of the century until the Lahti family bought it in 1915."

I perked up and looked at Maria and Alia.

"Toivo Lahti, a Finnish immigrant, moved his family from the Upper Peninsula of Michigan, where he and his son had worked in the copper mines. He got the stamp mill going again, first five stamps, then the other five. Things were going well until his son Eino was killed; the family said it was a defective blasting fuse. They found his body seven hundred feet into the tunnel buried under a foot of muck.

"Some people say it wasn't an accident—that it was murder. You see, the Lahtis' daughter had secretly married a partner in the business, and the family never approved of him. Albert Millerton, the partner, disappeared. After the tragedy, the family slowly lost interest, and the stamp mill has been closed ever since." Butch smirked and stared off into space for a moment. "There are a lot of stories like that . . . but let's go on to the stamps."

Down the stairs we went again to the bottom level, a big room where Butch pointed to the "stamps"—which were like solid iron potato mashers the size of dinner plates. Each thousand-pound stamp was connected to machinery that forced it down onto the rock, smashing it into powder. Butch said the mixture of fine quartz sand, gold particles, and water was then fed onto tables where it was screened and the gold recovered through amalgamation.

I perked up at that word, remembering it from John Cornwall's diary. Amalgamation, according to Butch, was the mixture of gold and mercury. The liquid mercury mopped up all the tiny gold particles like a sponge. Then the "sponge" was heated and the mercury evaporated, leaving the gold behind, looking like Swiss cheese..

"That's just about all, folks," Butch said. "You might want to look through our restored Assay Office. There's a guide there who can explain how the gold was processed. Any questions?"

I raised my hand. "Was anybody hurt in that cave-in the other day?"

"Hmm, I'm surprised you know about that. No, there wasn't. And, by the way, there's some thought that a bear may have triggered it."

"A bear? How cute!" said Maria.

"Not cute—they're dangerous. It's getting cold, and

they're getting ready to hibernate. Those tunnels"—he pointed up the hill—"are good shelter for them. So we don't advise you wander off on your own." He pursed his lips and crossed his arms.

Butch turned to talk with another family on the tour. Maria, Alia, and I walked back down around the front side of the stamp mill then stopped. The November wind was whipping down off the mountain, making the ponderosas softly whistle and sway. I zipped up my jacket. How could it get so cold when the sky was so clear and the sun so warm overhead?

I looked up the mountain and bit my lip.

Immediately Alia took my jaw in her right hand and turned my face toward hers. "Annie, don't even think about going up there. The man said there are bears up that hill. Big hungry bears that have a hard time finding lunch in November."

"Lunch?" Maria reached into her backpack. "I'm prepared." She pulled out four king-sized Snickers bars.

"One for Annie. One for Alia. One for me. And one for the bear."

I grinned, and Maria and I dragged Alia around the left side of the stamp mill, out of view of Butch and the others. There were rock tailings all around the building, so we had to be careful of our footing while we were off the path. We were just about out of sight when *Rrriiinnnggg!* What? *Rrriiinnnggg!*

"Annie, answer your backpack!" Maria whispered.

Rrriiinnnggg! I reached inside my pack and grabbed the

phone. "Oh, hi, Dad." I grinned. "It's Dad."

Maria and Alia grinned back. But not grinning was Butch, who had heard the phone and was storming around the building toward us.

"Okay, Dad. Gotta go. Right—visit Grandma Rose. Bye."

"I thought I warned you not to wander off this time of year," Butch said. "You're supposed to stay on the trails."

I looked left, then right. "You mean this isn't the Scenic Nature Trail? Jeepers, we were looking for the Scenic Nature Trail, right?"

Maria and Alia nodded on cue.

"Well, you're way off course," said Butch. "The trailhead is down by the museum. I suggest you follow me."

We meekly followed Butch back down to the log building. I didn't know how to figure him—not that he was opinionated or arrogant—but why would a guy like him volunteer at a state park? He was out of high school, and his mother couldn't make him. Maybe he was on probation performing public service hours!

"This is good," said Alia, as we entered the museum. "Much safer. The only bear in here is stuffed!" She pointed toward the natural science exhibit.

"More history credits," said Maria, picking up a free brochure.

I shook my head. History was the last subject on my mind. "We can check out those letters and things John Cornwall was reading." I waved them toward Henry's counter. "Sir, we'd like to see the old letters and diaries. We're doing a history project." I smiled and stood up straight.

Henry stretched too. "Well, I guess there's no reason why not. You ladies go right ahead. You know where things are. Everything might not be in order exactly. The museum director, Mr. Taylor, is making copies of all the papers and journals in case they were to get lost or damaged. But go ahead and use what's there—just be careful."

We found the research room and looked into the drawers. The original letters and old diaries were gone! In their place were spiral-bound paper books. I thumbed through one titled, "Letters of Louisiana Millerton." Inside were photo copied pages of the letters we had seen earlier.

"Look!" I said. "They're not gone—just copied. Maybe this will actually make it easier." We each took a book of writings and sat at a different corner of the table in the middle of the room. We quickly thumbed through the volumes, looking for three names—Millerton, Lahti, and Sierra-Eureka Mining Co.

"Annie, look at this!" Alia handed an opened book to me. It was the letter that John Cornwall had copied into his diary—from Sarah Millerton to her mother, Sirkka Lahti. As I read it over, I knew where John Cornwall had gotten his beautiful handwriting. His mother's was a piece of art.

"Can I help you ladies?" A tall, thin man in dark-framed glasses stood in the doorway coughing lightly. He wore khaki pants, a white dress shirt, and a navy-striped tie. An attempt to whisk his thinning hair over a large bald spot was less than successful. "I'm Carl Taylor, the museum director."

"We're doing a project for history. We're looking for letters related to the Sierra-Eureka Mining Co. Are they all here?"

"I've been making copies of all the primary source material in our museum," he said. "Eventually we'll have these organized better. There are several in that book you have there. And there are many in this book." He set down the box he was carrying and placed a book in front of me. "I'll put the rest in the fourth drawer and start working on the fifth drawer's contents. Please don't disturb any of the loose letters or original diaries. Happy reading. Let me know if I can be of further help."

I opened the book. The first letter read "Dear Mr. Millerton," and was signed by Toivo Lahti.

11

TUNNEL VISION

I motioned to Maria and Alia, and they gathered behind me. I took a deep breath as I opened the book, "Sierra-Eureka Mining Company Correspondence," and began reading the letter, written in broken English.

Dear Mr. Millerton,

As you have taken company funds and used them to reopen Tunnel No. 9 without approval, this letter dissolves partnership. I will give you nothing. Your contribution to partnership was to be lode mining expertise and labor. You do labor, but your expertise is worthless. My son Eino agrees. I write this letter twice so I have copy.

This is awkward situation, with my daughter Sarah enjoying your company. There are, I tell her, other suitors.

Toivo Lahti
June 15, 1920

I nodded. "So there was a falling out between Albert Millerton and Sarah's family."

"I wonder," said Maria, "how Albert took this. Is there a response? I turned the page, then a few more. "Here it is."

Dear Mr. Lahti,

You are a stubborn man. You depend on geologic calculations and human reasoning and find you are more often wrong than right. I depend on my God-given instinct and am usually rewarded. It is true digging this old tunnel out is taking time, but patience and perseverance are important in any new endeavor.

You cannot take my world away from me. I will continue to work on Tunnel No. 9, without your or Eino's help. But Sarah has agreed to assist me by becoming my wife and helpmate. As you read this letter that I am having delivered, we are becoming man and wife at the Budgets' home.

I am a stubborn man also, Toivo Lahti.

Albert Millerton

June 20, 1920

I flipped through the remaining thirty or so pages.

There was no more correspondence between Albert and Toivo—just other company business letters.

"Just two letters? Imagine that."

Maria and Alia smiled and on a silent cue crooned one of the latest country tunes: "Imagine that! Lovin' me more than his John Deere hat. Imagine that!"

I gave them the "cut" sign. They had promised not to embarrass me in public with their singing.

"Hey, we could look through the museum exhibits," said Maria. "More history project credit."

I stood up, putting the books away. "Maria, this case is more important than history. But perhaps there's something about the Lahti family or the accident there."

We stepped back into the center hall area near Henry's desk. I pointed to a sign to the right of the front door that read, "Stamp Mill Exhibit." We wandered into the room and to a large exhibit on the far wall that was a cutaway diorama of the mountainside with the nine tunnels, ore carts, and miniature men at work.

"There's the cave-in." I pointed to Tunnel Number 9, high on the right side of the mountain, closed off deep into the hillside.

We wandered into the front corner of the building where a miniature model of a stamp mill sat. "Push This Button," said the sign, so I did. THUNK THUNKETY THUNK. THUNKETY THUNK THUNK. The ten tiny stamps pounded as long as I held the button down.

I let go. "Boy, imagine that a couple hundred times as noisy. Look at this." I walked to a glass-cased exhibit on the front wall marked "The Sierra-Eureka Mining Company." In the exhibit were items from the Lahti family, including pictures, clothing, and other things like a shaving mug and brush, a gold watch, and a pocketknife.

"I wonder why these things didn't go to their family members," said Alia.

"Alia," said Maria, "they didn't have any family after Eino was killed and Sarah ran off with Albert."

The three of us paused in front of a newspaper article. The headline read, "MINE CLAIMS LAHTI SON IN COL-

LAPSE." The three-paragraph story didn't tell us anything new, except that Toivo Lahti shut down the stamp mill and ordered the dozen employees to help dig out his son. Operations ceased initially for a week, then permanently after another few months when the company went bankrupt.

Alia shook her head. "Sad story." She sighed.

"True," I said. "And it's all interesting, but we're not getting any closer to finding John Cornwall." I walked back to the cutaway diorama of the system of tunnels and stared at Tunnel Number 9. Maria and Alia followed and stood behind me.

"I have this gut feeling that there's something there," I said, pointing to Tunnel Number 9.

"Like Albert Millerton's 'God-given instincts'?" teased Maria.

"Yeah," I said, crossing the room and peeking out a small front window. "I think God is leading me somewhere."

"We're going to T-T-Tunnel Number 9?" Alia bit her nails.

"Yeah," I said, smiling. "I just want to make sure Butch isn't going there too."

12

CAUGHT!

I stopped at Henry's counter, picked up a copy of the brochure "Scenic Nature Trail" and dropped two quarters in the donations box. Outside we took one look right and left, and with no sign of Butch, started up the hill. With just a general sense of where Tunnel Number 9 would be, we followed a trail that sometimes dead-ended at a boulder or manzanita bush. Then we would scatter a few yards and pick it up again.

"Wow, this is some nature trail," said Alia, stooping down to pick up something. It was light brown, about an inch in length, with a cone shape.

"Alia . . ." Maria let out a slight gasp.

I looked at Alia and put my hands on my thighs to rest a moment. "Alia, this is not the Scenic Nature Trail. I just took that brochure to throw off Henry. Hey, that looks like whatever was on Butch's necklace."

"Alia . . ." Maria started again, "that necklace that Butch had was made of rattlesnake rattles.
That's a. . . ."

In one instant two things happened: Alia threw the rattle down the hillside, and I clamped my hand over her mouth to cover her scream.

"You can't scream." I shook my head. "Okay?"

Alia nodded slowly, but as I took away my hand, she still stood there frozen in terror, her mouth wide open.

"It's okay, Alia," said Maria. "The rattlesnakes are probably in hibernation. It's getting cold. Maybe we should go get it and give it to Butch as a peace offering."

But Alia turned around and headed upward. "Rattlesnakes, bats, and bears, oh my. Rattlesnakes, bats, and bears, oh my."

Maria and I picked up on the chant and followed Alia up the hill.

After twenty minutes we had lost sight of the stamp mill and museum grounds. Most of the pines had been logged for timber off the mountainside years ago to shore up the tunnels, but there were still a few trees and scratchy manzanita bushes that blocked our sight. It was tough climbing—greater than a forty-five degree angle, we agreed, at times.

The wind groaned around the mountain peaks. All of a sudden I realized that we were very alone up there, and that if something happened to us, we might not be found for days . . . or hours, at least. *God, is this what happened to*

John Cornwall? Did he head up here and meet with trouble? I looked around. We had wanted to follow his tracks. Had we?

Just then I heard footsteps. Not heavy, human-plodding ones, but light, scratchy ones. Something was just to our right, on the other side of a pile of large rocks. I motioned to Maria and Alia, and we climbed up the pile and peered over. Sitting in a small cleared-out area was a squirrel munching a dried berry.

I smiled. "Hi, fella." But the squirrel was not a tourist-seeking variety and seemingly disappeared into the hillside. I craned my neck and looked around the rock pile to my left.

I gasped. We were perched on the very edge of a mining tunnel! We scrambled over the rocks and stood under a wooden timber that read, "Tunnel No. 9—Kentucky Portal." I cupped my hands around my eyes and peered into the opening to the tunnel. Somewhat loose wire fencing blocked the entry. On the fencing a sign dangled: "DANGER! DO NOT GO BEYOND THIS POINT!"

Just twenty feet inside the portal the timbers on the right side of the walls were slumped; the tunnel was partly blocked off with rock and debris.

I tested the fencing. It gave under my slight pull.

"Annie, there are several good reasons not to go in there," said Alia. "Number one: Bears. Number two: A tunnel that caves in once could cave in again. Number three . . . uh . . ."

Rrrriiinnnggg! Rrriiinnnggg!

"Number three is that your backpack is ringing again," said Alia. She and Maria snickered.

I grabbed the phone. "Hi, Dad. No, I'm still at the stamp mill. And Dad? You'd be proud of me. I'm doing research for my history project. Yeah. Okay, I'll visit her this afternoon. You're right, Dad. Stay away from that cave-in area? It's dangerous? Right. Thanks, Dad. Bye."

"Number four," said Maria, "is that you just told your Dad you'd stay away from this place."

"And number five is that you were told not to come up here!"

We froze, then slowly turned around. Butch stood facing us, his arms folded across his chest.

13

RAVIN'
AND CAVE-IN

Butch ranted and raved all the way down to the museum. "The upper trails are not open to the public. The mine tunnels are dangerous. You were warned. I should call the police." I wondered if he had an Authentic Mother Certificate.

But the remark about the police reminded me. I hadn't checked with Deputy Sheriff Smithee in a while. Maybe it was time to hightail it down the hill back into town. We didn't dawdle. While Butch was in the middle of complaint number four hundred and four we jumped on our bikes and coasted down the road.

At the edge of town we paused at the two-lane bridge that crossed the Sierra River, looking for the source of a motor's hum. Just fifty feet to our left downstream we found the cause of the noise—gold-dredging equipment poised in the middle of the river, with cables holding it in place from both banks. Material was sucked into the equipment, and held on a small platform, where gold flakes were separated from other material.

A man in a full black wet suit stood in the water, which reached his knees as it bubbled over a rock-filled bed. I shivered. The temperature of that water had to be something close to the inside of a refrigerator. The man turned toward the bridge, noticed us, and stared back for a moment. Then he waved. It was Mr. Millerton!

He walked to the river's bank and motioned for us to join him.

"I don't think so," I muttered under my breath.

But Maria had turned her bike around to head his way. "C'mon, Annie. It'll impress him that we've been working on our projects."

"Oh, all right." I followed Maria back around a dirt driveway that led to an informal parking area next to the river. We dropped our bikes and walked to the river's edge.

"I guess your elbow wasn't broken, just bruised. Is it feeling better?"

Millerton smiled. "Just bruised. I expected to see your grandfather here this morning, Annie, but not you."

"He's not my grandfather. He . . . he's just a friend of my grandmother's. And, actually, he's kind of missing."

Millerton's jaw tensed. "Missing? That's odd. Come to think of it, I thought he was going to call me last night about the claim. Is there a problem, do you think?

Something I could help with?"

"You could just keep your eye out for him," I said. "You haven't noticed any signs of him around the river—any of his personal things or equipment?"

Millerton shook his head. "There wouldn't be much. He was just panning—for the fun of it , you know, nothing serious."

His dredger started to chug, then shut off. "Oops, gotta go. Hey, Annie, I misunderstood about John. He talks about your grandma a lot. I just assumed they were married. Rose—isn't that her name?"

I nodded.

"He talks about you, too. Said the other day that he appreciated your interest in history." Millerton laughed. "That was a good one, huh—interest in history?"

I forced a laugh. "Yeah, right, Mr. Millerton."

Maria stepped right next to me and took my arm. "Well, as a matter of fact, Mr. Millerton, we've been working on our history projects all morning."

Alia took my other arm. "That's right. We've already visited two museums and taken the stamp mill tour."

I sighed. It was good to have friends. A couple months back I'd been the new girl in town and totally friendless. Then I met Maria and Alia.

We said our good-byes to Mr. Millerton and in a matter of minutes were cruising past the "Welcome to Mountain Center" sign. We agreed that one-and-a-third Snickers bars was not enough to sustain us, so we parted ways until after lunch.

I stopped at the sheriff's department. Deputy Sheriff Smithee said bulletins had gone out with no reports back. "It's going to be tough. With John's truck parked in his garage, there's got to be a local connection somehow. We just haven't figured it out yet." He picked nervously at some lint on his shirt, then looked at me. I knew he knew we girls had solved a couple of cases a few months back.

But I shook my head. "We haven't found out much, either. In his free time he was doing some gold panning and some research on his family." I thought a moment. "Oh, his bike turned up at the Quick Save yesterday."

"His bicycle?" Smithee pulled out a spiral pad and pen.

"Yeah. A volunteer at the stamp mill said Mr. Cornwall left it there, but it turned up at the gas station. Weird, huh?"

"Maybe some kid stole it, then had a change of heart."

"Maybe." Or, I thought, someone was trying to throw off a scent away from the stamp mill museum.

Smithee said he'd tried to look up Cornwall's family but ran into a dead-end. "He just doesn't have anyone, that we can tell." I nodded. I knew he didn't have any brothers, sisters, or children. "He's a private man, it seems. Volunteers at the church a lot, but doesn't talk much about himself."

Just then the dispatcher called Smithee out on an emergency.

But I'd had an idea. There was someone who knew Cornwall better than others: Grandma Rose. I stopped at the hospital on my way home. She was sitting up in bed, sipping hot tea that sat on an otherwise untouched lunch tray. Sitting in a chair on the other side of her bed was Dora. I cringed. I did not want Grandma Rose stressed out by Dora's talk about John Cornwall being "all she had."

"Hi, Grandma Rose. You're looking perky." I tweaked a half-hearted smile through gritted teeth. "Hi, Dora. How nice of you to visit."

Grandma Rose reached over for a hug. "Hello, Anne dear."

Dora stood up. "Isn't this a shame—your grandmother laid up like this. And Mr. C. still missing. Things come in threes, come in threes. What next? What next? " Dora kept murmuring to herself.

Oh, brother. I knew what was next. "Dora, thanks for visiting Grandma Rose, but she needs to finish her lunch."

Dora left the room murmuring, "the only one I have" as she nodded and waved absentmindedly.

"That woman does not look well," said Grandma Rose. "I'm concerned about her."

"Grandma Rose, you're the one in the hospital bed. You just worry about yourself." I sat down on the bed and pushed her tray closer to her. "Now, eat some of this."

I sighed as I watched her pick at the sort of yummy-looking chicken and rice. I thought of all the times when she had served me tea and health cookies when I was upset. Now I was trying to help her. Life sure could turn around quickly.

The food seemed to calm her and she began to talk.

"John is a most unusual man. He's curious and considerate to a fault. If something's broken, it becomes a challenge to him to see if it's fixable. If someone has a need, he's there to help. If there's a question or a problem, he digs to the bottom of it."

"That's why he was researching his family?" I asked.

"Yes," said Grandma Rose. "I think, down deep, John felt that if there had been a problem in his family, he wanted to know what it was so he could make it right." She shook her head and looked at me, sighing. "That's the kind of man John Cornwall is."

I gave Grandma Rose a hug. She said she would probably be in the hospital another day—until the doctor felt confident about her medication. I told her I would visit her the next day, Sunday—either at home or in the hospital before she was discharged.

As I was waving good-bye, Mom and Dad walked into the room. I smiled at first, but they both had a troubled look in their eyes.

"Mom? Dad?"

Dad removed his baseball cap. "Annie, have you heard?"

I shook my head, looking at Grandma Rose. "No, what?"

Dad cleared his voice. "There was another cave-in on the mountain—an explosion in one of the tunnels. A hiker was hurt, and they're bringing him into the hospital right now."

14

A VISITOR

Mom hugged me. "We heard a news bulletin over the radio and were worried. We knew you were up there. And you didn't answer the phone—I guess you had it turned off."

"We called the stamp mill museum," Dad said. "And talked to someone. . . ."

"Henry?" I asked.

"Yes," said Dad. "He said three girls had gotten into trouble." He looked at me.

Mom wiped her eyes. "You were snooping around the tunnels, Annie? That's what the man told Dad."

I nodded slowly.

"Annie! You could have gotten hurt. And we've been worried to death. We've been looking for you all over the place."

After all the what-ifs, I put my bike in the back of Dad's pickup truck, and we went home for lunch. As I munched my ham sandwich and chips, I could not get past one singular thought: Something weird was going on at the stamp mill. A cave-in and an explosion within a day of each other at a mining site that had not been worked for over seventy years? I didn't know much about mining, but that seemed odd.

"Annie, would you please check the message machine? Let us know if there's anything important, okay?" Mom was eating her sandwich on the go as she and Dad were heading back to the feed store. "And stick around, please. We really were frightened."

"Right," said Dad. "It's okay to be a sleuth, but dead isn't couth."

I rolled my eyes. Dad's attempts at humor were usually corny.

They were driving down Fairgrounds Alley when Maria and Alia knocked, then walked in the front door. Rusty welcomed them with enthusiastic wags and lots of licks. A watchdog he wasn't. I waved them into the kitchen, pushed the play button on the message machine, and picked up pencil and paper.

Beep. "Hi, Link. It's Crystal. Call me when you get home from work."

I rolled my eyes at Maria and Alia. A no-brainer. What else would Link do when he got off work?"

Beep. A hacky, deep cough. "Stay away from the mountain. Accidents happen."

Gulp. I set down the pencil.

"That was definitely a threat." Alia bit her lip.

I tapped my forehead. "You know, it may be good news, though."

"That we're on the right track?" said Maria.

"Yes," I said. "We're obviously pushing someone's buttons. Let's go see if we can figure out who's wearing the shirt." I erased the messages.

Listening to our answering machine reminded me that we hadn't checked John Cornwall's, so we pedaled there first. I knocked on the back door, just in case he'd returned, then entered.

I looked around. There was no sound. I checked the answering machine as Maria and Alia looked over the rest of the house. There were three messages, the first two from Grandma Rose and Dora. I waited for the third with my pencil and pad.

Beep. "This is Julie at Melvin C. Smitherson's office. We have your claim papers ready. Please call the law office at 231-1200 for an appointment. Thank you."

I hastily jotted down the number and name.

"Claim papers?" Maria had reentered the kitchen with Alia following her. "Do you think he's actually filing a gold claim?"

"He had that book about filing claims on his desk, remember?" I said. "And he's been panning regularly. Maybe he found something big."

"Well, we came on something big." Alia held out several pieces of mail. "Look what I found just inside the mail slot on the floor."

Whew! Looking over someone's mail was a pretty personal thing.

Maria must have read my mind. "Look, Annie. We've broken into the guy's garage and home. We've read his appointment book and his journal and listened to his answering machine. We've even taken his dog! If he's in trouble, maybe something in the mail will give us a clue."

I flipped through the mail. A magazine. A credit card offer. The phone bill. And a postcard. I turned it over and read aloud: "Your recent order is ready to be picked up. Thanks for your patronage—Mountain Designs Jewelry."

"Does he wear a lot of jewelry?" asked Maria.

"No," I said, setting down the mail on the kitchen counter next to the phone. "I've never noticed any. But he was teasing Grandma Rose about having rings made from the gold he panned. Maybe he actually did it."

"Maybe you're right, Annie. Maybe he really did hit something big out there on the river," said Alia.

"Yeah," said Maria. "And maybe we need to go visit Mr. Millerton again."

"I don't know." I headed for the door. "Here's a theory. Suppose John Cornwall quickly became quite good at gold panning. Suppose that he even found a good source by the side of the river."

Maria and Alia nodded as they followed me out.

I walked toward our bikes. "Suppose he had a dispute with another miner or miners and decided to file a claim. Remember the threats?"

"We're with you," said Maria as she straddled her bike.

"Then Cornwall disappears. Who would have motive, means, and opportunity?"

"One of the miners?" Alia said.

"More specifically," I demanded.

Maria's and Alia's jaws dropped at the same time, and they said, "Mr. Millerton?"

I half-smiled and nodded smugly.

Maria shook her head. "I don't think so. A school-teacher? Don't they take an oath or something?"

I chuckled. "You're thinking of doctors. Besides, if John Cornwall was kill . . . hurt, who else have we run into that would have a reason?"

We all stood there staring into space for a few moments.

"Butch!" said Alia. "I don't trust him. He's . . . he's mean."

"The young prospector at the river that Cornwall wrote about in his journal—the guy with the leathery skin," said Maria. "He said someone threatened him—remember?"

"And then there's the voice on the tape," I said. "We just have to figure out who's got a nasty cough like that."

Maria snorted. "About everyone in town. It's that time of year. Even Henry does and Dora, and the museum director, Carl Taylor."

Ah, ah . . . choo!

We looked up. Walking down John Cornwall's drive-way toward us was a young man wearing faded jeans and a blue work shirt. His dull brown hair was disheveled, and his skin was sun-worn and cracked. He pulled out a well-used red bandana and wiped his nose.

"I'm looking for John Cornwall," he said.

15

NOT SO
CRYSTAL CLEAR

"Mr. Cornwall is not here right now," I said. I was thinking of Mom's what-to-say-to-strangers lecture.

The man put his hands on his hips. "Well, where is he? And who are you?"

"We're friends." Maria put her hands on her hips and stepped forward. "And you should identify yourself first."

"He's buying me out. Claim, equipment, everything. And he owes me some money." The man looked about nervously. "We were supposed to meet yesterday, but he didn't show. I just want my money, then I'm out of here."

"Sorry I can't help you, sir," I said, moving slowly toward the front sidewalk. "If I see Mr. Cornwall, I'll tell him to get in touch with . . . what did you say your name was?"

"Jim Dirk. D-I-R-K." He walked toward the faded blue Volkswagen bus that was parked at the curb, coughing into his bandana. "He knows where to find me. And he'd better soon." He climbed into the van, started the engine, and quickly drove off.

"Jim Dirk? Dumb jerk!" said Maria. "I'll remember that name."

"That's not nice," said Alia. "Hey, let's go get an ice cream cone before we go back to the stamp mill. My treat."

Maria and I did not take much convincing, and soon we were cruising Main Street downtown. The Sierra Pharmacy with its soda fountain was just across from the courthouse. On the way we slowed past several antique stores; it was fun looking at the old things in the windows. Just then a familiar form came shuffling down the street: Dora. She was carrying a flat wooden box that tinkled as she walked.

We coasted to a stop and pulled our bikes up onto the sidewalk to say hi. It would be sort of hard for anyone to miss three girls blocking your way on the sidewalk, but she did. Instead, she turned left into the New Thought Bookstore.

We girls turned and looked at each other. We knew something about the New Thought Bookstore from an earlier case. Joanna Bentley ran the store that catered to cultists and New Agers and their hunger for books and objects that emphasized individual power.

Dora? A New Ager? She looked more like an old ager.

We walked our bikes to the display window. Jazzy yet classical-sounding music that reminded me of wind chimes floated out the open door. A banner hung across the inside of the store: "Leaders of a New Age: Develop self-mastery and find universal harmony."

I looked over at Alia. She didn't like this place, either, I could tell. She was praying. I decided to do the same.

God, I haven't been a Christian very long, but there's one thing I do know: You are the source of power. You are the master of the universe, and only in You is there harmony. Please protect us while we enter this place.

"Let's go in, said Maria, starting for the doorway.

"I don't think we need to," said Alia with new confidence. "Let's just see what she's doing from here."

I nodded and we peered from behind book displays in the windows. Dora was talking with the owner, Joanna Bentley, who stood behind the checkout counter. Dora opened her box, then held up two clear crystals that were the length of her pinkies and were curled upward. Joanna Bentley took them in her hands, nodding admiringly, and then set them back in the box, pulling it toward her on the counter. From a drawer below the counter, she counted out several bills. Dora folded the money twice and stashed it in a small coin purse that she slipped into her dress pocket. Then she started back toward us.

"Let's get out of here," I said, jumping onto the seat of my bike.

But just at that moment Dora looked up, as did

Joanna Bentley. And from the corner of my right eye, I saw the mouths of both of them drop in surprise.

16

FOUND
AND LOST

To throw off Dora, I led Maria and Alia into the alley behind Sierra Pharmacy, and we entered through the back door. We walked through the narrow aisles and sat at the three end swivel stools at the luncheon counter. There were always four flavors: vanilla, chocolate, strawberry, and the flavor of the week. I always ordered the flavor of the week.

An ordinary-looking high school girl stood behind the counter with scoop in hand and a bored expression on her face.

"Single scoop of rocky road in a cone, please." I smiled to make her smile. No doing.

Maria and Alia ordered the same, and the girl slowly filled our cones and brought them to us. Alia plunked three dollars down on the counter, which the girl ignored.

Instead, she sighed and slowly began wiping the other end of the counter.

"So," said Maria, "why would Dora be selling crystals to the New Thought Bookstore?"

"She must be into that New Age stuff," said Alia. "Joanna Bentley seemed to know her. I bet she goes there a lot."

I shook my head. "It's hard to imagine. But I guess anyone can be misguided if they don't have a personal relationship with God."

"I don't see anything wrong with crystals," said Maria. "After all, didn't God make them? I have a pair of crystal earrings at home."

Alia turned on her stool. "God made crystals. But New Age people believe crystals have healing powers. Imagine a rock healing someone. My Rock is my God, the Healer."

"I agree, " I said. "I don't want anything that could be associated with a cult or the New Age Movement. I wouldn't want anyone to think I promoted that kind of thing."

We finished our cones on our way to the county park. We agreed that we needed to see the explosion firsthand. I called Mom to let her know where we were going.

"Be careful, Annie," she said. "Use your head."

Push. Push. Pedaling up the mountain for the second time in one day was rough. It reminded me to keep bugging Mom and Dad about a horse—not that I would take one up such a steep hill. They said the horse would be a reward for working at the store and getting good grades. But with my 'D' in history? Maybe not.

Push. Push. Whew! The road leveled out at the parking lot of the stamp mill museum. I looked up at the mountain. Billowy white clouds were whisking over the peaks, and the wind was whooshing down the face of the hillside. I pulled my jacket around me. Was a storm coming in? No, those are white clouds. It'll be all right.

"What are you staring at, Annie?" asked Maria.

"I'm wondering if John Cornwall is up there somewhere." I bit my lip. "If he were following a lead in one of those tunnels, maybe he's there. Maybe he's behind that caved-in tunnel. And maybe it wasn't an accident. Maybe he found out a family secret that someone didn't want known, and maybe that someone triggered the landslide."

"That's a lot of maybes, Annie," said Alia.

"Maybe not," said Maria seriously.

Alia snickered, then laughed out loud, and Maria and I joined in. As we parked our bikes, Deputy Sheriff Smithee came by in his white squad car. He waved and rolled down his window.

"You girls be careful. We're not sure what happened here today. We think an old dynamite charge further closed off Tunnel Number 9. That's the tunnel that buried the owner's son years ago. Kind of spooky." He grinned. "Or, you never know, this might be where California splits in two and falls into the ocean." He laughed heartily.

Ha, ha. I'd lived through a major earthquake in L.A., and it was not funny. I'd heard there were earthquake faults all up and down the Sierra. Could a plate shift cause a cave-in?

"Sir, this may sound wild, but do you think Mr. Cornwall could be trapped up there? He's been hiking around here regularly."

Smithee looked over his left shoulder up the hill. "That's a good thought, young lady. A cave-in and an explosion? I'll follow up on that." He tapped his cap with his finger. "Our Search and Rescue Team has a specialty unit for mine rescue. We'll see what they can do."

As we stood on the sidewalk, a boy about a head shorter than I dashed from behind us to a woman exiting the front door of the museum.

"Mommy, look what I've got! A crystal! I found it on the mountain!" He held it in his palm.

A crystal? This was a too-weird coincidence. I motioned for Maria and Alia to jog with me over to them.

"Excuse me, could I see that?" I asked. "We're kind of interested in crystals." I held it up. It was like a prism—clear, six-sided, and about the size of my pinky. At that moment the sun peeked from behind a cloud and its light diffused colors through the crystal's sides.

"Cool!" said the boy. "Lemme see!"

I gave it back.

"That's neat, Timmy," his mother said, "but when you find something like this in a park, you can't take it home. This is its home; it needs to stay here."

We followed them back into the museum, the boy grumping behind his mom. Henry was on duty again at the greeter's counter.

The lady walked her son over to the counter. "I'm sorry,

sir, but my son picked this up on the Scenic Nature Trail. He didn't know better, so I thought I'd bring it to you."

Henry cleared his throat. "Well, yep, that's a crystal from one of the tunnels. Wonder how it got out on the Nature Trail. Peculiar thing. Maybe a critter carried it. I'll just see that the museum director gets it to the right display. Thank you, ma'am, for your courtesy. That was mighty neighborly of you."

Henry set the crystal in a glass case below the counter where books and souvenirs such as mini-gold pans and arrowheads were on display. The woman and her son left, and we were about to head outside when Carl Taylor called out.

"Ladies, I've got something that might interest you here. It's from the Lahti family."

He handed me another spiral-bound book of copies. On its cover it read, "Sirkka Lahti's Journal."

I looked at Maria and Alia. Maybe this journal would reveal the secrets that the mountain was hiding—how the Lahtis' son was killed and what other heartaches divided them from their daughter, Sarah. I glanced at my watch. It was almost two o'clock. We had most of the afternoon to read it, but something up on the mountain was calling to me.

God, is that You nudging me?

"Mr. Taylor, thank you, but I feel like a good hike." Maria and Alia gave me a "Huh?" look. They were not up to a good hike. "Can you tell us where the Scenic Nature Trail starts?"

He took back the book. "Sure, you can go right out the front door and follow the trail to your left. It winds up a ways and then to the left of the stamp mill. Better make it a short hike, though; I hear there's a storm coming."

Maria followed me, but Alia dawdled as we walked out the front door, whimpering like a puppy.

"Annie," said Maria, "that journal—it's a good lead."

"Yeah, Annie," said Alia, "I'm kind of pooped. I know, why don't you two take a hike while I read the journal. That way we can cover two territories at the same time."

I shrugged my shoulders, and Maria nodded.

"And, Annie, guess what?" whispered Alia.

"What now, Alia?"

"That crystal that Henry put under the counter? It's gone—I took a double look just now."

I looked at Maria and gulped. Could Henry have given it to the museum director or filed it away somewhere? No, there hadn't been time.

I shook my head and sighed. We checked our watches and agreed to meet back at the museum at three-thirty.

Maria and I started toward the mountain when Maria stopped and said, "Oh, Alia, if you hear an explosion, bring a shovel, okay?"

I scowled at Maria. There were five hundred and five reasons why that was not funny. And she knew it.

17

A FIND

Maria and I started for the Scenic Nature Trail. We looked around to see if anyone was watching, then headed around behind the stamp mill and up toward the tunnels. Rocks—from pebbles to fist-size and larger—now littered the centermost part of the trail, which zigzagged up the hill. I kicked them as we trudged along, Maria leading the way.

"Ow! Annie, do you have to do that?" Maria rubbed her right leg.

"Sorry, Maria. I'm checking for signs of John—a swatch of clothing, dropped paper—something, anything." I continued to kick along the trail.

"Well, you go first, then!" Maria pulled my arm, then pushed me ahead of her.

"Whoa! Maria!" I tripped off the narrow trail and started sliding on my bottom down the hill.

"Help!" The loose rock of the hillside kept me from catching hold until I'd slipped about twenty feet from the trail. There a luckily placed timber lying flat stopped me. My feet hung over its edge. As I looked out a little, I realized it was a good thing the timber was there, since it was perched at the edge of a straight drop.

"Annie! Are you all right?" Maria slid down next to me and hugged me, holding me back off the edge.

I nodded. Straight drop? I peeked over between my knees to the space below. Sure enough, I was sitting on the top of . . . I read the sign upside down . . . Tunnel No. 5, Tennessee Portal.

"Maria, it's another tunnel!"

"Well, let's check it out!"

We carefully climbed down from our perch, holding onto shrubbery as we slid along.

"Yeow! Where were you, manzanita bushes, when I was bouncing down the hill?" I rubbed my elbow where it had brushed against the scratchy greenery.

It was not surprising that we hadn't spotted this portal before: A ponderosa pine and some manzanitas had grown just below it, enough to make it hidden from any distance other than close-up.

But someone knew it was there. As we faced downhill, a small path led down and to the right away from the opening.

Only a foot's width, the path was worn down and the dirt soft; someone trekked to the tunnel regularly. The same wire fencing and warning sign greeted us as the one at Tunnel Number 9: DANGER! DO NOT GO BEYOND THIS POINT!

"I wonder why we haven't come across more tunnels as we've climbed this mountain?" said Maria. "Aren't there supposed to be nine? This is only the third we've seen."

"Well, I think Butch said something about closing some of them off when they'd been worked out," I said.

I cupped my eyes and peered into the portal.

Maria did, too. "So, if this wasn't closed off, there could be something worth getting in there?"

I didn't answer. I had seen something at the edge of the tunnel's darkness—a lighter spot than the pitch black nothingness. I tested the stubbornness of the fencing by pulling on it. It gave away immediately, surprising us both, so that we bonked heads as the wire sprang toward us.

"Ouch! Annie! Was that payback?" Maria rubbed her head.

"Sorry again, Maria." I pushed the fencing to the right side of the opening and took a step inside.

"Annie, there's been a cave-in and an explosion in the last two days—both unexplained. Are you sure you want to do this?"

It was too late. I was already doing it. I slowly inched my way into the tunnel. Something was up against the right wall just ahead of me.

Maria crept along behind me. "Annie, that thing up

there—it's sort of human-looking." She'd seen it too.

As the darkness began to envelop us, I wished I'd had a flashlight in my backpack. I turned toward the tunnel's opening. Very little daylight was visible through the brush and tree just outside the portal. And I was beginning to feel closed in overhead. Is something breathing on me? Is this tunnel alive? I reached up cautiously to test for the top of the tunnel, still looking at the thing, which was almost at hand. We inched, inched when . . .

"Aaaggghhh !" Maria and I both screamed at the same time.

Something was flapping against our faces and hair. We instinctively ducked and squatted, holding our arms over our heads.

"Aaaggghhh!" I continued to scream. I grabbed for Maria and she grabbed for me. We both fell to the ground, our arms around each other in fright. It was like a ride on Space Mountain at Disneyland—things flying at us left and right in the dark—except we weren't moving.

As quickly as it had started, the flapping stopped, but every ounce of my flesh was trembling.

"Annie, stop!" Maria shook me. "They're gone, Annie!"

I opened my eyes. "I d-d-don't even want to know what they were."

"Annie," said Maria, "you don't know? Those were just some of Bert's cousins."

"Bert?"

"You know; Bert the bat. And I guess we can tell ol'

Butch that the Townsend Big-eared bat is not as endangered as he thinks it is."

I took a deep breath to calm myself. Just a bat. It was just a harmless bat. I shivered again. Just a bat? Good thing Alia's not with us.

In any case, we found we were squatting right next to the "thing," which turned out not to be a human, but a man's coat on a hook that must have once been to hang a mining lantern. I reached up and pulled it off the hook and held it at arm's length with two fingers. No telling what other creatures might be hanging out in it.

"Sure is, and I don't think a miner left it here. It looks fairly new. But I can hardly see a thing. Can you see anything else here?"

"Annie, all I can see are the whites of your eyes and the portal opening. Let's get out of here."

Maria led the way out, carefully so as not to disturb the bats, which were hanging out at the tunnel's opening, waiting for us to leave. *Next time we come here*, I thought, *I'm bringing a flashlight . . . and an umbrella!*

Getting out just took seconds. At the portal's opening we sat on a boulder and looked at the navy zip-up jacket. It was a little dusty, but it obviously had not been there long. I looked at the label at the neck—nothing but laundry instructions. But along a side seam there was another label. It read, "This belongs to," and written in pen was, "John Cornwall."

18

BENCHED

"Annie, someone's coming." Maria's eyes darted about.

Sure enough, there were voices coming up the path. We scrambled down the hill and hid behind the big ponderosa pine that blocked the entrance. The voices grew closer and closer. They sounded familiar. I clutched at the coat, and Maria hung onto me as we both squished behind the tree.

The voices stopped at the portal. I couldn't stand it. I had to peek around. Butch was pointing into the tunnel; Mr. Millerton was standing behind him. With the wind whisking down the mountain and the men facing the tunnel entrance, I couldn't hear all of their conversation.

". . . safest spot . . ."

" . . . good choice . . ."

". . . let me know soon . . ."

" . . . I owe you . . ."

Just a couple minutes later the two headed down the hill again, and we shifted around the tree to stay out of their view.

"Annie, what have those two got going, do you think?"

"It sounds like they're in a partnership for something," I said. "And that Mr. Millerton owes Butch—something."

Maria wanted to follow them—the girl had no fear. But I didn't want to risk another run-in with Butch. Instead we climbed back to the upper path, then and hustled down behind the stamp mill and into the museum.

Butch and Mr. Millerton were chatting just inside the front door.

"So your old man was in mining?" Butch looked at Mr. Millerton with a nod of respect.

"And his father before him." Mr. Millerton shrugged his shoulders. "It's in our blood, I guess."

"Hope there's no blood over this escapade," joked Butch.

"Yeah," said Mr. Millerton. "It's always possible when you're dealing with kids." He looked up as we passed. "Oh, hello there, young ladies. Well, Butch, thanks. I'll talk to you later."

Just then Carl Taylor fumed out of his office on the far right side of the building. "Butch! Henry! I've got a problem."

The three men gathered in the front hall area. "Search and Rescue is bringing in a backhoe. They say there could be a man buried in that cave-in on Number 6. Smithee says a man's been missing in Mountain Center—John Cornwall, the director of the county museum. It's preposterous! Henry, didn't you tell me you had that cave-in checked out?"

"Why, yes, sir," said Henry. "I called a mine rescue unit and a feller came with his sound-detection equipment—said he couldn't hear a thing. And with no sign of anything unusual, we just left her be." He scratched his head. "John Cornwall? Isn't that the same guy . . ." He looked at us. "Why, these here gals have been looking for that feller, too."

All three men stared at us.

"What do you have to do with all this?" Carl Taylor's veins were popping out of his neck.

"Sort of nothing and everything, sir," I joked. "Mr. Cornwall is a friend, and we've been trying to find him. It seems he's been visiting the park and museum lately. And . . ." I decided to come out with it. "As a matter of fact, we just found this jacket of his up on the mountain."

Butch snorted. "Up on the mountain? Where? I check the trails regularly, and never saw it. And what were you doing up there? Didn't I tell you to stay off the trails—that there are foraging bears, dangerous things? We had an explosion today, for goodness' sakes." He paced one step to his left, then one to his right, then back again.

"Well, we started out on the Scenic Nature Trail." That was not a lie; we did. "Then we found our way to Tunnel Number 5, where we found the jacket."

Carl Taylor was tapping his fingers together. "You found the jacket outside the Tennessee Portal?"

I bit my lip. "Well, no. . ." I winced and half smiled. "We found it in the tunnel."

"In the tunnel?" all three men exclaimed.

"In the t-t-tunnel?" Alia had joined us. "You w-w-ent in the tunnel?"

"Just a little," said Maria. "The jacket was hanging on a hook. We didn't go any further, and we didn't disturb anything."

Butch sputtered. "Didn't disturb anything. Sure. You must have moved the wire fencing and the sign that tells you not to enter."

Carl Taylor grunted. "Well, I don't have time to deal with you girls. Just sit there a minute until I think this all through. I've got the whole Search and Rescue crew coming—and probably every fireman in the county. Brother! They'll tear up the whole park before they're done." He stormed out the front door.

Butch followed him. Henry shook his head at us and resumed his post at the counter. We sat on a long bench that lined the center wall.

"Annie, you're not going to believe what I found," whispered Alia. "Sarah Millerton wrote two letters to her mother. I copied them. Look."

Maria and I scrunched in close to Alia on either side. She held up the little notebook that I had given her, and we read Alia's handwriting:

Dear Mother,
Time is passing. I know you want to write to me, but that

Father would not approve. I hope you receive this letter. I ache from loneliness. There is no word from Albert. As I have no means to support myself, I have given my son to a fine family in Placerton. All I have is this big empty home that I cannot sell, as it is in Albert's name as well as mine. I have no family. May I come see you?

      Love, Sarah

"That is so sad," Maria said. "No family. I can't picture a life with no family."

"Yeah," I said. "You have a zillion relatives, huh, Maria?"

She nodded.

Alia flipped the page. "And here's the other one—this is what's really interesting." She read:

Dear Mother,

    I read in the newspaper today of Eino's death. Do you think so little of me that you would not even tell me about my brother dying? It was hard enough when you turned me away at the door. This increases my pain to where I can see no hint of hope.

    People say cruel things, Mother. Are they true? Some say Eino was seen with Albert that same day, and that they had argued. Others say Eino was drunk and deserved to die—that the cave-in was his fault, because he was target shooting in the tunnel.

    I am still not certain why Father will not see me. My husband is gone; his child is gone. I am still your daughter. Will we all die because of the mill? Why don't you end all this suffering by selling the mill? I believe that it has an evil hold on you. Please implore Father to release the grip of death that mountain has on our family.

In spite of everything, I am grateful that I still have a heavenly Father who loves me.

Love, Sarah

"Do you think John Cornwall read these letters?" Maria asked.

Alia's eyes flashed. "I looked in the checkout book. He did—on Thursday."

"Two days ago," I said. "The day he disappeared."

19

DIGGING TO
THE BOTTOM

"Annie, did you hear Mr. Millerton and Butch talking about kids and bloodshed?" Maria whispered into my ear.

The whispering didn't work: Alia heard. "Bloodshed? Annie, you're not paying me enough for bloodshed."

"Alia," I said, "I'm not paying you anything."

"That's exactly what I mean!" Alia pushed up her gold frames.

"Maybe," I said, "those two had something to do with John Cornwall's disappearance. If they know we're after them, maybe they'd resort to drastic measures to protect themselves. Maybe we even need some kind of protection."

"There's Rusty," said Maria, "or Bear."

I smiled. Bear was Maria's poodle/shepherd one-year-old puppy. He was a little dog with a big growl.

"That's okay," I said. "We don't need Bear. We have Someone watching over us."

Just then the whole parking lot filled with large-engine sounds. I looked over at Henry, who was seated at a desk behind the counter, flipping through a magazine.

I tiptoed to a front window. A large truck was trailering a backhoe. I assumed it was a backhoe, anyway, because the truck cab sign read, "Sam's Backhoe Service." Also pulling into the lot were pickups with yellow-coated men, an ambulance, and a fire engine. Jumping out of a small blue sedan was Maggie Lewis, news editor of The Mountain Center Messenger; I'd written a couple features for her after our last case.

Hmm, maybe she knows something.

I gestured with my finger, and Maria and Alia tiptoed beside me. Henry still had his back turned. I gave them the "wait" sign; then, when the next beep-beep of backing equipment sounded, we slipped out the door.

Carl Taylor was angrily directing traffic. The truck driver had pulled through the lot and stopped, and an equipment operator in well-worn jeans was driving the backhoe off the trailer.

"Go away—you'll tear up the mountain!" Butch was yelling, flapping his arms, and running back and forth between men gearing up with shovels and other hand equipment and the equipment operator.

"Boy, he's upset," said Maria. "Think he's trying to hide something, Annie?"

"Anything's possible. He and Carl Taylor must have a

pretty good reason for not wanting things disturbed."

All of a sudden, Carl shouted, "No, I won't! Why don't you ask them?" And he pointed in our direction. I turned around. There was no one behind us.

Then Carl slipped over to Butch, who was near us now, and said, "I'm going into town to get help. I'll see if I can get an injunction to stop all this."

"Annie, is that legal stuff? An injunction?" Maria asked.

"Yeah," I said. "It's a court order that could stop the rescue effort."

Butch headed into the museum, and all eyes focused on us.

Deputy Sheriff Smithee walked over. "Well, ladies, we understand you found something of Cornwall's today. That jacket his?" He pointed to the jacket hanging over from my right arm.

I held it out. "Yes, sir, it's his—it's got his name in it."

"We can take you to Tunnel Number 5," said Maria.

He smiled. "Well, let's go then."

In minutes a long procession of Search and Rescue men and women, fire fighters, deputies, mine rescue team, the ambulance crew, Maggie Lewis, and the backhoe operator was winding its way up to the Tennessee Portal. Alia, the numbers girl, said she counted twenty-nine rescuers in all, plus us. The people had to find a resting place away from the portal, as the equipment operator had to rest on the flat space for digging.

But first the mine rescue workers set up listening

devices against the rock spill and hushed everyone else so they could hear. Within minutes a tall, thin man with thick glasses pronounced, "I hear something. He's alive in there!"

The mine rescue team quickly assessed the spill and gave directions to the equipment operator on how to proceed. The hillside, the man said, was vertical slate, naturally unstable and further decomposed by exposure to the mountain weather. "The rest of this whole section could come down on us," he said, waving toward the hill.

I bit my lip. Then I pulled out the phone from my backpack.

"Hey, Annie, no fair calling in a story." Maggie Lewis moved next to me. She had her pen and notepad poised. "I've got the radio guy beat on this one. I can't beat him in our paper since we're only a weekly, but I can call it in to the wire service."

We smiled at each other. I could see how being a reporter was sort of like sleuthing. "Digging to the bottom of this one, Maggie?"

She groaned, and so did everyone around. But it was clear that small jokes did not help much. The life of a man was at stake in this rescue—perhaps the lives of each of us standing there under that unstable mountain.

I dialed. "Hi, Mom. Just wanted to let you know that the rescue people are at the stamp mill. Yeah, they think—we think he could be behind that cave-in." After six hundred and six questions, I put the phone away. Mom said she thought she'd wait before telling Grandma Rose.

There was no telling what we'd find beyond, or underneath, the rock.

Slowly, tediously, the operator pulled at the edges of the cave-in. As he did, many with shovels also probed at the rock debris. One load was dumped down the hill. Then another. Then many more. Minutes passed.

I bit my nails. Suppose we found him—dead. Suppose nothing was beyond the rock. Suppose it had just been my wild guess. I clutched at the coat, sighing. John Cornwall, I don't know if I want them to find you in there or not. I glanced at my watch. It was 3:28. We'd been there almost an hour.

Just then a crew of two huffed up to the dig scene. A husky, ponytailed man carrying a large camera followed a tall man with plastered blonde hair.

Maggie Lewis frowned. "Oh, great. So much for a scoop. It's Channel 3."

20

UNBEARABLE

It didn't take the Channel 3 reporter long to find out that I was behind the rescue effort. One finger after another pointed down the long line of folks standing on the mountain path—right in my direction. The reporter inched by them with the cameraman following.

"Hi there. Troy Durant, Channel 3." He stuck out his hand.

I took it. "Annie Shepard, After School Sleuths." I bit the inside of my mouth to keep from grinning.

Maria and Alia rolled their eyes and shook their heads, trying to inch away. But I pulled them to either side of me and introduced them.

Troy pulled a pencil from behind his ear. "So, I understand this," he pointed to the digging backhoe, "is all your idea."

I scratched my chin. "John Cornwall is a family friend. He's been missing since Thursday, and we've been trying to find him. He was last seen here at the park." I held up the jacket. "This is his coat; we found it in a tunnel today."

He grinned. "So you're a little Nancy Drew group, huh?"

I cleared my throat. "Mr. Durant, we may just be kids to you, but we've solved two cases in the last two months. And . . ." I looked over at Maggie Lewis. "See that reporter over there?"

He nodded.

"I have an exclusive agreement with her. She's working for the Associated Press." I smiled. "So I don't think I should be talking to you right now. Bye!" I scooted past a couple firemen.

Maria pulled on my elbow. "Annie, you could have been on TV. Why'd you dump that guy?"

"Maria, there are some things that are more important than fame and fortune."

"Like?"

"Like respect." I patted her on the back. "Besides, I think we'll be on TV anyway. The cameraman was filming."

Another hour passed as the reporter wandered from one worker to another, interviewing, taking notes. Then he paced up and down the trail for a while, glancing at his pad and talking into space. The cameraman was taking a nap against a boulder off the trail.

Alia pointed. "He's getting ready for 'Live at Five.'"

The minutes ticked off as the workers dumped shovelful after shovelful of rock down the hill. We sat down, watching the men chip away at the mound of rock and dirt.

"I can't believe this is taking so long," said Maria.

"Yeah," I said, "it's longer than waiting for the bell in history class."

"Well, I'm sorry you feel that way."

I turned around and looked up. Oops! Mr. Millerton stood over us with his hands on his hips. I forced a grin.

"What's going on here?" he asked.

I took a deep breath, then told him how we'd followed John Cornwall's trail to the stamp mill museum and how we'd read his journal and the diaries and letters.

"Hmmph. Amazing. I didn't think you girls were that interested in history." He walked away, shaking his head.

I blinked and stared as he shuffled down the path. Interested in history? Teachers could be so . . . so confusing. I turned around and watched the rescue. Now, that was something interesting: action, excitement, adventure. History in the making!

History in the making? I thought about how Toivo Lahti had bought the Sierra-Eureka Mining Company. That one seemingly ordinary event—buying a business— had affected the lives of many others. It provided jobs that drew families to Mountain Center. Miners had a certain derring-do fiber in them, I'd learned, that was admirable—a willingness to chase after a dream.

Living in the mountains required, even today, a certain

fortitude. Families still had to sacrifice bigger cities' opportunities and wealth for small-town benefits like safety and a sense of belonging. Perhaps those original miners left behind their "why not?" attitude for all of us who followed.

I sighed. I understood what Mr. Millerton meant. Reading diaries and letters of our local forefathers was studying history. I smiled. Maybe studying people's lives and trying to undertand why they did what they did wasn't so bad after all.

Behind me, coming up the hill, a bunch of cussing grew louder and louder. I stood up. Jim Dirk was waving his arms at nobody in particular.

Deputy Sheriff Smithee put his hand up. "Hey, got a problem?"

Dirk frowned. "You bet I do. You guys are chasing an old guy in a mountain when I think he's just skipped town. He owes me money—cheated me out of a claim. This is a waste of time."

Dirk started to threaten the deputy sheriff with his fist, then backed off when he realized he was overpowered.

"Keep an eye on that character," Smithee said to a deputy who'd been coordinating the shoveling crew. "I'll take your place for a while."

Troy Durant wound up his soliloquy to the rocks and motioned to the cameraman to follow him to the front of the portal.

"It's live," Maggie said. "They rushed a satellite over from Reno."

The cameraman and Troy took a firm stance. Lights were now set up, the sun having slipped behind the mountain. I glanced at my watch. It was 5:02. Troy nodded and pointed. The cameraman began shooting.

"Yes, Bart, we're live in Mountain Center as a brave crew of dozens continues to chip away at a mining cave-in. Local authorities, tipped off by a young girl, believe a local museum director, John Cornwall, is behind the tons of rock and debris at this mine entrance . . ."

I grimaced. Soon thousands would know about me, Annie Shepard, and the After School Sleuths. Hmmm, maybe my friends in L.A. would see this. . . . Fame? Fortune? I shrugged my shoulders. Maybe that wouldn't be so bad.

Troy continued. "Ah! It looks as though the hardworking crew has just this moment broken through."

I gasped. The backhoe operator turned off the engine and jumped down as several of the workers also ran just below the portal timbers. They pawed with their shovels at the last bits of rock. It was true! They had cleared a small opening!

"Stop! Stop that, I said!"

Pushing his way through the crowd, with the cameraman catching it all on camera, was Carl Taylor, waving a piece of paper in his hand.

"I've got an injunction!" Taylor yelled. "It's all legal. I'm Carl Taylor, the museum director. The judge signed a temporary order. Stop defacing this park and leave this instant!" He pushed the others away from the mine entrance and stood facing all of us.

Troy wasn't missing a beat, almost. "Uh, Bart, it seems a museum official, Carl Taylor, has an official court order here stopping the rescue. Uh, from what I can gather, he's upset about the environmental effects this equipment could have on the park. And, uh, oh, dear!"

I looked toward the portal. Deer? It wasn't a deer at all! Climbing out from the small hole in the cave-in wall was a large bear.

21

NO CHOICE?

Carl Taylor sensed something was wrong and turned around quickly. Spotting the bear, he scrambled back with the crowd which was inching away.

The bear blinked its eyes and cocked its head as it sniffed around and uninterestedly eyed the crowd. Then, just as leisurely as it had squeezed its way out, it retreated back into the tunnel.

Carl, red-faced from both the quick hike up and the embarrassment, stood before the crowd. "Okay, that should settle things. John Cornwall's not in there; it was a bear. Everyone go home now." He waved his hands toward us. "Just go home."

Troy Durant signed off and gave us a dirty look as he rushed by. "A bear! Now they'll stick me after Whit the Weatherman next hour." The ponytailed cameraman laughed and strolled after him. So much for Channel 3.

The workers slowly gathered their equipment and wound their way back down. We did, too, pretending we didn't notice their smirks and pointing fingers. I shivered.

Darkness was settling, and the cool air was quickly turning cooler. At the parking lot we decided a drink was in order before we left for home, so we headed up the museum walkway behind another group.

Rushing out the door as we were about to enter came Dora. "Terrible. Just terrible." She wrung her hands together.

"Dora?" I waved slightly.

"Oh!" She started. "Oh, isn't it terrible?"

"About . . ." I wasn't sure.

"Why, about not finding Mr. Cornwall, of course." She looked at me questioningly. "You're going to keep looking."

I wasn't sure if it was a question or a demand. "Yes, we will."

She hadn't waited for an answer but had scuffled off, twisting her hands and muttering to herself.

We followed another crowd into the museum.

"Annie," whispered Alia, "look!"

Henry was leaning over the counter and talking with Jim Dirk. Fortunately, neither noticed us, and we tiptoed to the left exhibit hall. The three of us lined up just around the corner near a tunnel exhibit, trying to hear their conversation.

". . . and you close at six?" Dirk said.

"Five," said Henry. "We closed at five. I'm trying to finish up here now, so I can . . ."

"That's sure nice of Dora—coming here to check on John Cornwall," said Alia.

"Sshhh," said Maria. "I couldn't hear what he said."

Dirk took a look one way, then the other, and headed out the door. Henry walked into the other exhibit room and guided the group that had entered with us toward the door. Then he went back into the room and began straightening chairs and turning out the lights.

"Annie, I don't think he knows we're still here," said Maria.

I turned to look at her, but my eye was caught by the small-scaled tunnel diorama behind her. Behind glass, it was cut away like a large ant farm. I touched the glass at Tunnel Number 5, where we'd found John's jacket and witnessed the bear rescue. To its left was Tunnel Number 6.

I traced all the tunnels and shafts with my fingers, trying to memorize the uneven pattern between the three levels.

"Annie," said Alia, "you're not thinking of doing what I'm thinking you're thinking of doing." She looked at me with sad puppy eyes.

But I gritted my teeth and nodded. The tunnels and shafts all connected. John Cornwall might not be in Tunnel Number 5, but he might be in another one. With all the rescue folks leaving, we were the only search party left.

All I needed was a flashlight.

22

CRYSTAL SURPRISE

Gulp. "Mom! What are you doing here?"

Mom was walking up the museum sidewalk as we were leaving. Her work boots and jeans were dusty, and her pageboy had lost its perk.

"I was just able to get away from the store. Did they find him?"

I told her the whole story.

She sighed. "Well, I think your grandmother would want us to be optimistic. After all, he could have been found under the rubble."

I nodded.

She looked at the sky. "It's getting dark, Annie. Time to get home. Are you on your bikes?"

Home? I didn't want to go home. "Well, yeah, but . . ."

"I'd haul all three of you and your bikes home, but I

don't have room in the cab." Mom thought for a moment. "Annie, why don't you come get the flashlight out of the truck. It'll be safer for you on the streets."

I smiled as Mom got the flashlight out of the truck. Someone was watching out for me. She handed it to me.

"Now be careful. I know you're responsible, Annie, but other people aren't. Just watch where you're going." Mom waved. "See you at home."

I stared at the truck's tail-lights as Mom drove off. Maria and Alia had gone to get their bikes. Then I stared at the flashlight a moment. Would it be more responsible to go home or to follow a strong hunch that could save a man's life? What if John Cornwall were in that mountain? How long could someone survive without food and water? I couldn't remember—two days, four days? What if he were hurt? What if . . .

"Annie, you're not still thinking of going back in that tunnel, are you?" Alia was straddling her bike. "There's a bear up there! Get a grip, girl!"

"Yeah, Annie," said Maria. "Crystal clear picture here. We should . . ."

"No," I said. "Mom expects me to go right home. I wouldn't want her to worry."

"HELP! Help !"

A faint cry echoed off the mountain. I looked around.

Everyone had vanished. The shadows of two cars were visible at the end of the lot furthest from the road, but there was no sign of anyone else. Even the museum lights were now off, and Henry apparently had gone home too.

"What was that?" said Maria.

"I heard it too," said Alia.

"HELP! Help!" It echoed again.

"It's someone on the mountain," I said. "Someone needs help. We're the only ones around. It's up to us, After School Sleuths. Are you with me or not?"

"But what about your mom?" Alia asked.

I bit my lip. If someone were really in danger, my folks would be the first to step in and help if they were nearby.

"I'll call." While Maria and Alia dropped their bikes, I started up the hill, punching in the numbers on the phone. No one was at the store. No one was home. I left a message, explaining the emergency.

Maria and Alia dropped their bikes and followed me as I ran back up the hill. The large, boxlike flashlight lit up the whole ragged trail ahead of us as we followed the sound to Tunnel Number 5. In Olympic time we paused, huffing, at its portal.

"I don't hear it anymore, Annie," said Maria.

We walked slowly into the tunnel as I swung the light left and right, up and down. I hadn't forgotten that the ceiling was a living organism.

"Must have been a mirage," said Alia.

"Alia," I said, "you don't hear a mirage. You see it."

Alia was staring. And pointing. "Like that?"

Alia was right. Maybe thirty or forty feet ahead of us in the tunnel was a soft light. I looked at Maria and Alia. Where would a light be coming from? Could John Cornwall be in there after all? Was it his voice? I shined the flashlight on Maria's, then Alia's face.

"Well? Are you with me?"

Maria nodded slowly, then smiled. Before Alia could protest, Maria grabbed her by the arm and started singing, "Are you with me, though we fight? Are you with me, through the night?"

By the second line, Alia had joined in the tune. Some of the Townsend's Big-eared Bats apparently didn't like country music, however, and fluttered the other way out the entrance. That was all right with me, as long as they were going the opposite direction.

With the flashlight guiding us, we quickly found our way to the conductor of the light—a shaft that opened up on the left wall. We leaned over and stared into the opening. The soft light was stronger at the lower level. Someone or something was definitely a level or two below us.

I scanned the flashlight over the shaft. Heavy timbers, like those that lined the tunnel walls and ceiling every few feet, also lined the shaft, creating a ladderlike stairway.

"Ohhhhhh."

"That was a moan," said Alia.

I took off my backpack, dropped it to the ground, and stuck the flashlight in the waist of my pants. Then I eased myself down and caught the first timber, holding onto the opposite sides with both hands. I eased myself down again and found the next one, then the next.

"C'mon guys, you can do it too. It's really not that hard—oops." My flashlight had caught on something and pulled out from my waistband. We all groaned as we heard it smash on the rock, surface below.

Maria followed me, slowly finding her footing.

"Annie," said Alia.

"Yeah?"

"Well, whatever. I mean, I do not want to stay up here by myself. Look out below." And she started down too, saying, "I hope we can get extra credit for our history project for this."

After several minutes of descending, I heard a sound.

"Shush! Listen!"

Just beneath us were voices.

"How much further, Annie?" asked Maria.

I started down again. The light was getting brighter and brighter, seemingly warming up the shaft. I'd heard that the temperature in the mountain was a constant forty degrees, certainly warmer than the near-freezing temperature outside.

I stopped and looked down again. Was it possible that we'd reached the floor? The bottom level of the mining operation? It had to be: Rail tracks were just outside the shaft. The miners would have dumped the quartz rock down into ore carts, which would move along toward the stamp mill for processing.

Confident that earth was below me, I swung out of the shaft and stared into the lit room before me.

"WOW!"

Maria dropped beside me, then Alia.

"Wow!"

"Wow!"

Before our eyes was a wall-to-wall-to-ceiling crystal palace. We were standing at the edge of a two-storied room that sparkled like the inside of a geode. And waiting in front of us was Jim Dirk.

23

THREE-WAY TROUBLE

"Welcome to the vug," Dirk said.

"The what?" I slid out of the shaft and into the sparkling crystal room. Maria and Alia followed me.

"He said 'vug.'" Henry walked out from a corner, his hands full of crystals, which he set gently in a towel-lined cardboard box. He didn't seem surprised to see us—only perturbed.

"This crystal room is a vug." He gestured. "And you snooping little ladies have found it. I had a feeling it could come to this." He glared at us.

My heart was pounding, and I tried to breathe in and out slowly to quiet my nerves. Just when I thought I was recovering from my initial shock of sliding into New Age heaven and finding Dirk and Henry there, another crystal-laden figure stepped out from the shadows. It was Dora.

"Dora?" I exclaimed. "What are you doing here?"

Dirk gave a low laugh. "Well, it's not a meeting of the Mountain County Docent Society. And I've got nothin' to do with this guy or his nutty sister except business. Mining business."

Sister? Dora was Henry's sister? Mining business? Suddenly I understood what the three of them were doing: they were harvesting crystals out of the mine and selling them to the New Thought Bookstore. I had a new thought of my own. Maybe they were selling them elsewhere, too.

Dora must have read my mind. "You three snoops have ruined everything. What are we going to do, Henry?"

He patted her on the back. "I'll think of something, Dora. We don't want an accident again."

Accident? What accident? John Cornwall? Maria gripped my right arm. Alia gripped the left. She started whispering the Lord's prayer, her spiritual defense . . . or offense, depending on how you looked at it.

Oh, Lord, help me get a grip here. I have a feeling that we need to get out of here, and quickly.

"Well, folks, uh, sorry for dropping in like this." I forced a chuckle and started walking backward, easing Maria and Alia with me. We kept inching until we stood back on the rail tracks, just below the mine shaft opening, which headed back into a tunnel. "We'll just leave you to your, umm, business and . . ."

Dirk charged my way. "Hey, where do you think

you're going? You can't leave now that you know what we're doing. You're going to have a little accident, just like that old geezer."

"Geezer? I'll show you who's a geezer." And out of a tunnel opening came John Cornwall pushing a tilted ore cart straight at Jim Dirk.

We jumped back to the tunnel wall, but the movement caught Dirk by surprise, and he tripped trying to move out of the way. BAM! The cart rammed into him, and Dirk fell into the cart.

"Ohhhhh. Help! Help!" Dirk's weight in the cart kept it moving down the tracks toward a tunnel exit, picking up speed a little until we heard a . . . THUNK!

"Guess he's taken care of for a while." John Cornwall limped into the crystal room and sat down.

"Oh, Henry, Henry, Henry!" Dora was pacing. "I think we should . . ."

"This has gotten a lot more complicated than you said it would, Dora. I wish I'd never found this place. If only I hadn't stumbled across that entrance." He shook his head, pointing across the room.

"And worse, I wish I'd never told you about it. You just kept getting me deeper and deeper in trouble. You thought this vug had mystic healing powers. You thought meditating would make John Cornwall fall in love with you. Dora, you're nuts! I'm out of here!"

Henry stomped off toward the back wall, mumbling to himself and fluttering his arms. The movement sent flickering sparkles in waves over the walls and ceiling.

"Henry! Henry! Wait, Henry!" Dora shuffled after him, tinkling as she moved, her coat pockets obviously filled with crystals. "Oh, here's a good one. And another one. Henry, wait!"

John Cornwall stood up, holding his leg and wincing. "Annie Shepard, how on earth did you ever find this place?"

I smiled. "Mr. Cornwall, there's quite a history behind that." I smiled at the word "history." I was beginning to think that maybe history was kind of an exciting thing, especially around Mountain Center.

Mountain Center? I gulped. We were still in the center of the mountain and had to find our way out. I sighed. I knew God had a hand in our historical adventure and that He would see us back to daylight . . . or, at least, starlight.

I looked at John Cornwall really carefully. He sure looked good to me.

He smiled. "Annie, would you think me forward if I gave you a hug?"

Maria and Alia chuckled.

"No, sir. No, I wouldn't at all."

24

SMILES

Sigh. A hug in a vug. I smiled as John Cornwall patted my back. Maria and Alia were grinning too. I bet they knew at least three country songs appropriate for that moment. And I was sure they'd let me know at least one of them later.

I looked around at the vug and I laughed. It wasn't mystical, but miraculous. It was God's version of the Crystal Cathedral. Instead of mesmerizing New Agers, maybe instead, tourists could view this and come to know The Rock who created it.

"Annie, I don't feel so good," said Alia suddenly. "Sleepy or something." She yawned.

Maria looked rather dreary, too.

John Cornwall's eyes searched the room and looked troubled as they landed on me again. "We've got to get out of here. If they've closed off the entrance, the air won't be able to circulate. There . . . might be . . ."

I knew he was weighing his words, and I knew why. "Carbon monoxide?"

He nodded.

"We could climb back up the mine shaft," Maria said.

I looked at John. "Mr. Cornwall, did you hurt your leg?"

He lifted his tan slacks on his right leg. His ankle puffed his white sock out. "I think it's a sprain. From Tunnel Number 5 I found my way to Tunnel Number 9." His eyes saddened. "Inside the cave-in there—the one that killed Eino Lahti—I found what I think are my father's remains. It was hard to tell with only a flashlight, but I believe he died from a gunshot wound." He pointed to his forehead. "There."

"Eino Lahti killed your father?" Alia asked.

"That's what I'm guessing. The noise probably triggered the collapse that killed Eino. I found a letter at the museum." He smiled. "We'll have plenty of time to go over all that later."

"But your ankle—how did you . . ." I said.

"Dirk heard me in the tunnel and searched me out. He led me down here. He pushed me along and on the way I tripped over some tracks and twisted my ankle. I don't think he really meant to hurt me, but he was worried about what I'd do about them pilfering these crystals from a public park."

"But what did they intend to do with you?"

"I think they were going to let me go. They just wanted to clean out as many of the crystals as they could first and then leave town. They weren't bad to me. They brought me food and untied me to eat. That's what I was doing when you girls literally dropped in here."

"And who yelled help?" Maria asked.

"Dora," he said. "She was yelling at the other two to help her reach the biggest crystals. Then Henry slipped and moaned. Could you hear all that?"

I nodded.

But where was the way out? I looked around the brightly lit crystal cave. The light bounced like a magnified kaleidoscope. I looked at the beaming sources—three trouble lights hanging from opposite points in the vug. Brain wave! "Mr. Cornwall, where is this light coming from?"

"Well, it couldn't be a generator, because we'd hear the motor." He scratched his head. "Annie! It would have to be electricity, wouldn't it?"

I'd already guessed that and was heading for the closest light, hanging to our right. Sure enough, there was a long orange cord dangling from it and leading off across the room. I picked up the cord and walked along it, letting it run through my fingers. John Cornwall followed me with a hop hop, limping, with Maria and Alia behind him. One minute, two minutes, maybe five, we inched along that cord, taking us further away from the sparkling room and into the darkness again.

It grew colder and colder as we walked, with me at the

lead and the others shuffling behind me. Then all of a sudden the cord had no give. It was seemingly going into the ground, and I bent over to follow it, when . . . UGH! My head bumped into a wooden wall.

I straightened up and rubbed my head.

"Was is it, Annie?" John Cornwall stood next to me in the complete darkness.

"There's a wall or barrier or something here. I can't go any farther."

I heard John Cornwall run his hands over the wall. "It's plywood, I think."

Alia whimpered. "They've nailed it shut?"

"Let's put some buff into it," said Maria. "You know, try to knock it down."

I moved over and felt the others line up with me along the wall. A faint glimmer of light peeked through in spots around the edge of the plywood wall. What could that be?

"Okay," I said, "one, two, three, UGH!"

We pushed with all of our might and WHOA! The whole sheet of plywood gave way, and we tumbled down onto it. As we stood up, we found ourselves looking right into the bright lights of Camera 3 "Live at Six."

25

MYSTERY IS HISTORY

All the time I lived in L.A., I thought I wanted to be on television. I never fancied myself as a sitcom beauty queen—more like the friend next door. You know, the funny one. But with lights and a camera right in my face, I went totally dumbstruck. All that Troy could get out of me was an occasional "uh-huh" and a rather lame grin. If that weren't embarrassing enough, my whole family was there too, hugging me and stuff, right on camera.

During Troy's interview we did find out a few details: When I didn't return home, my parents called the sheriff's office. They and a new rescue party, led by Carl Taylor, found my backpack in Tunnel Number 5. Taylor then led the group to the portal of Tunnel Number 2 where they caught Dirk dazed in the ore cart and Henry and Dora nailing shut the plywood entrance. Dirk told them everything, trying to place the bulk of the blame on Henry and Dora. He even admitted that he had tricked John Cornwall into buying his claim by planting some gold flakes and a nugget. Dirk had caused the cave-in and explosion to frighten us off, and he took John's bike to town. Henry—as a daily museum volunteer—would have known when the coast was clear, when he and Dora could enter the tunnel without being seen. When the camera lights pulled away, I got my bearings quickly. We were standing on the tracks that led to the stamp mill trestle, the same spot we'd been yesterday when we took the stamp mill tour.

"Kate, Mark," said John Cornwall to my folks, "this daughter of yours and her friends saved my life. She is one amazing young lady. But you already know that."

Mom had one arm around me. Dad was on the other side. They put me in the middle of them and scrunched me like a hamburger between two buns. More embarrassment, but I figured I'd live.

Four men—Dad, Link, Butch, and Carl Taylor—helped John Cornwall down the hill to the museum parking lot. In the lot Deputy Sheriff Smithee was helping Henry, Dora, and Jim Dirk into the white patrol Jeep. As we followed them, I learned that Butch was a college student— a history intern at the park. He was responsible for educational tie-ins to the park, including the arrangements for a student tour for Mr. Millerton, which we had overheard earlier. So much for "kids and bloodshed"!

Dora was yapping at Henry in doubles. Dirk, his head

between his knees to cover his ears, was cussing.

Henry, red-faced, finally turned to Dora and said, "Dora, just zip it!"

Smithee shut their door and turned to me. "Great detective work there, Miss Shepard, Miss Miller, Miss Martinez." He shook all our hands. "You rescued John Cornwall, nabbed three thieves, and discovered a natural treasure for Mountain County. Personally, I appreciate it. And I can't wait to see that crystal room for myself."

"What'll happen to them?" I still couldn't believe that museum volunteers could deface a public park as they had done.

"That'll be up to the District Attorney," he said. "From what Dirk says, they've been cleaning that place out for a couple weeks. At the least I think restitution and some public service are in order. Don't you?"

I nodded. "Sir?" I had suddenly had another thought.

"Yes?"

"Do you think the vug—the crystal room—could be the lost Mountain Center fortune?"

"I wonder." He rubbed his chin. "Folks always thought the treasure was a big vein of gold. Maybe it was actually the crystal room. You know, Annie, you may have solved one of the local history mysteries."

We shook hands with him again, said good-bye, and headed for our bikes.

All of a sudden I paused. One of the history mysteries? Could he mean there were more? I looked at my friends as we climbed on our bikes.

"Annie, I know what you're thinking," said Mari__

"So do I," said Alia. "You're thinking that there might be other history mysteries around here, huh?"

"Well . . ." I said, pulling my bike out of the rack.

"Forget it, Annie," said Maria, "at least for a while. At least until we solve the mystery about how to get our history project done."

I didn't say anything. I just smiled. And at that moment a few light flakes began to fall. Snow? In November? Wow! I caught one on my tongue.

Thanks, God!

We followed the entourage of Channel 3, the sheriff's Jeep, and other rescue folks back into town. I met Mom and Dad at the hospital where they helped John Cornwall get emergency care for his sprained ankle. After X-rays, bandages, and crutches instruction, he met us in Grandma Rose's room.

They kissed and hugged, and my face reddened again.

"I have a proposal," he announced.

"What?" I said.

"Not for you, young lady," he said. "You've had enough action for a while." He turned to Grandma Rose. "For you, Rose." He took her hands in his. "Will you do me the honor of becoming my wife?"

She sighed. I sighed. Mom, Dad, and even Link sighed.

"'I could not love thee (Dear) so much, Lov'd I not honour more,'" she recited. "Richard Lovelace—and that means, 'yes,' by the way."

John Cornwall smiled. "I'm glad that ring I've ordered

won't go to waste. Does that mean you'll be my new guide, too?"

Grandma Rose laughed. "You mean I'm a two-fer-one deal?"

"Well, not exactly," he said.

"Oh, Gram," I said. "Why not? I mean, museums are pretty cool places. They've got lots of history and stuff in 'em."

Everyone turned and looked at me as though they were meeting me for the first time. And then we all had a good laugh. I guess I had learned a new appreciation for history through the whole adventure. And I guess the lesson was timely, since John Cornwall had just learned that Mr. Millerton was his cousin. Their fathers were brothers. I figured I was surrounded by history, and I'd better learn to like it. In fact, I'd even volunteer as a guide at one of the county museums.

It was like that verse that John Cornwall wrote in his diary: "You have given me the heritage of those who fear your name." I had learned that studying history and the Bible could teach me a lot—even about myself.

The best part of the day, though, was Troy's sign-off in his Live Action 3 report. The nurses let us stay, and we all watched it on Grandma Rose's TV.

I giggled as I watched Troy put his arm around my shoulders and say into the microphone and camera, "Well, Bart, that's about all here in Mountain Center. I'm signing off for Live Action 3 and," he smiled at me, "Annie Shepard and the After School Sleuths."

Now if that wasn't the best way to impress a history teacher, I'm not sure what is.